A FAITHFUL BRIDE FOR THE WOUNDED SHERIFF

BEAR CREEK BRIDES BOOK TWO

AMELIA ROSE

CONTENTS

This book is dedicated to all of my faithful readers, without whom I would be nothing. I thank you for the support, reviews, love, and friendship you have shown me as we have gone through this journey together. I am truly blessed to have such a wonderful readership.

CHAPTER 1

$\mathcal{J}$enny Jenkins lay in the bed that she and her husband had shared for the last year and a half. Pain swept over her body in waves as the time had come for her to deliver her first child. It was late in the evening when Jenny first felt the pains of labor, and as soon as her water broke, Mathew had raced into town to collect Dr. Harvey. Now, Jenny labored in bed next to her mother who had come to support her through this major trial.

Jenny had to admit that she was quite terrified of giving birth. She had heard the horror stories of women dying in childbirth in the West because remote locations often lacked the modern medicine that she was used to in the East. But with her mother by her side and a very reassuring Dr. Harvey, she was confident that soon she would be able to give birth to her and Mathew's first child.

"Just keep breathing, Jenny, and soon this little girl or boy will be here," Dr. Harvey encouraged. Another wave of pain crashed over Jenny's body as her stomach constricted and urged the newborn forward. Jenny held tight to her mother's hand as she tried to breathe through the pain.

"That's it, my dear," Margret said as she sat on the edge of the bed and tried to comfort her daughter. Having only had one child, it had been a while since Margret had remembered the pains of childbirth. She only hoped that Jenny would be able to endure them and remain relaxed.

"Just think about how happy you're going to be once you're able to hold that baby in your arms," Margret said in a comforting voice. "I'm excited to see my first grandchild, so don't take too long." Despite her pain, Jenny chuckled. Margret moved to the water basin on the dresser, dipped a cloth into the cool water, and returned to her daughter's side to dampen her hot forehead. Giving birth was exhausting work and already they'd been at it for over three hours.

Margret did her best to push back Jenny's auburn hair from her face. It was hard when Jenny would become restless and try to move into different positions. The whole time, Dr. Harvey remained patient as he guided Jenny the best he could. They were still waiting for the baby to crown, and since Jenny was giving birth for the first time, it could yet be a while before any progress was made.

"I never knew it would be this hard," Jenny said as she lay on her side and tried to catch her breath after another wave of pain subsided.

"It will only be for a short time, my dear. Then you'll feel all the joy in the world," Margret encouraged. She'd helped Jenny into a night-gown, but because it was late spring, the weather had warmed up quickly, making the room humid. Margret left her daughter's side for just a moment as she went to the window and pushed it open, coaxing cool air to enter.

"Ah, that feels much better," Jenny said as she rolled onto her back. "I think I want to stand by the window for a bit." Margret then helped Jenny over to the window. She peered up into the night sky. "Looks like it's going to be a full moon tonight."

Dr. Harvey chuckled as he glanced out the window as well. "Seems like the perfect night to have a baby," he reckoned. "Nothing says new beginnings like a full moon." Jenny thought she liked the sound of that as another wave of pain came through her. She gripped onto the windowsill and did her best to take deep breaths through the pain. At this point, all she cared about was delivering this baby and not being in any pain anymore.

Margret rubbed her daughter's lower back, hoping to keep her as relaxed as possible. There were no maids or servants to help with the delivery. And though she and Jenny had become used to living in Bear Creek, Montana, sometimes Margret missed aspects of her old life, where money hadn't been an issue. But Margret pushed the thoughts of the past out of her mind as she focused solely on her daughter and grandchild.

~

MATHEW JENKINS WAS out on the front porch with his cattle dog, Bailey. He'd been pacing back and forth along the wooden boards for the last few hours, waiting as patiently as he could to hear the news that Jenny had successfully given birth. He ran his fingers through his shaggy brown hair for what was probably the hundredth time as he did his best to keep his nerves under wraps. The last thing he wanted to do was add to Jenny's burdens.

"Come, Mathew. Let us play a game of knuckles," Brown Bear encouraged from where he sat in a rocking chair. He was petting Bailey as he watched Mathew pace back and forth. He'd come the moment the Great Spirit had urged him to visit Mathew immediately. He was pleased to hear that Jenny was finally having her baby, but poor Mathew wasn't dealing with the waiting part very well.

"I don't know if I want to play right now," Mathew mumbled as he continued to pace. He wrung his hands together, wondering if perhaps he should try to take a peek to see how Jenny was doing. But then he doubted himself, thinking that Dr. Harvey and Margret would be able to handle things. Mathew didn't like waiting when something this important was about to happen. He longed to hold his child and was full of fear at the same time for Jenny's health. He was doing his best to keep all negative thoughts out of his mind but couldn't help that sometimes they snuck in there from time to time.

"I could set up some targets and we could practice our aim," Jacob Benning offered. He was perched on the front steps of the porch. When Mathew had come riding into town at a fast pace and he heard that Jenny was in labor, he'd collected his horse from the livery stables and rode out with Mathew and Dr. Harvey. Jacob was excited for his best friend and had come to support him. But what the Sheriff of Bear Creek had failed to understand was how long it took to give birth.

"I don't think Jenny would appreciate all the gun fire," Mathew reasoned as he looked to Jacob during one of his paces on the porch. "But I appreciate the thought."

"Hey there, Boss," came the voice of Peter Gibson as he walked up the front lawn towards the ranch house with his partner, Bobby Lukens. They were two young men from the next town over who had answered Mathew's post for help wanted on the ranch. Now, the two young men helped Mathew out with the herd that had doubled earlier that year. Jenny and Margret had made an investment in the ranch and, so far, that investment had been paying off as spring came and the cows began to give birth.

"Hi, Peter. Bobby," Mathew said as he stopped for a moment and looked at the two cattle hands. "Everything okay out there?"

"Yeah, Boss. Nothing to worry about. Only have about four cows left that still need to have their calves," Bobby said, his southern accent strong. They had told Mathew that they had previous experience working in Texas, but had moved north when their previous boss had been bought out. As long as the two did their job well, Mathew hadn't really worried about their past.

"Sounds good, boys. I appreciate you two keeping an eye on things while I'm here at the house," Mathew said. It was prime birthing season and he sounded worried that the two cattle hands would be disappointed in him for not sticking with the job.

"The herd is in good hands, Boss," Peter said as he slapped Bobby on the back with a broad smile. "We've been doing this job since we were old enough to ride a horse.".

The sound of singing then filled the night. Jacob looked to the west, and saw torches and ponies coming down from the mountain and out of the forest. Brown Bear stood with a smile on his face as he called out to his people, the trill of his voice rising up into the air. Mathew shushed him, but the Sioux Indian Chief paid the man little attention as several Indian maidens came bearing baskets of something that smelled delicious to Jacob.

"It seems like the party is only getting started," Jacob said as he stood to his feet to witness the small group of Indians coming up to the house. It was late at night and he was famished from having skipped dinner to come straight to the Jenkins' household. And as the air filled with the savory smell of food, he was grateful for the maidens bringing it all this way from the Indian camp deep in the mountains.

"Greetings," Brown Bear said as he hopped over the side of the porch and approached the party. "Thank you all for coming to support Mathew and Jenny."

"Come now, Chief. We have only come to make sure you eat something, but made certain to bring plenty for everyone else," one of the maidens said as she slid off the back of the Indian pony while still safely holding the basket in her hand. She handed it to the chief with a dip of her head. Brown Bear removed the top of the basket and looked at what it contained.

"Here we have fish and root vegetables; let us eat," Brown Bear said as he turned back to the others. He handed the basket to Mathew, who sat in his usual position in the rocker.

"I often help in the house," Mathew murmured to Jacob as he was given a wooden trencher, "but in Indian culture, it is the woman's responsibility to cook and serve the men, so I don't want to offend these lovely maidens by offering to help here." He waved at the others to sit on the porch steps and allow the women to serve the food.

"Thank you," Mathew said and tried to eat a few bites of fish with his fingers. Jacob could see that his mind was with his wife as she struggled to give birth to his child.

"I've never had fish before that wasn't fried," Bobby spoke up and smirked, as if to say that things were done a bit differently in the south.

"What do you mean you've never had fish that wasn't fried?" Jacob responded, finding the statement surprising. "What about baked fish or grilled fish, or even fish casserole?"

"Nope. My mama always fried the fish me and Daddy would catch on Sundays," Bobby admitted as he took a few hesitant bites of the fish. He seemed to like it enough as he continued to eat with his fingers.

"Well, it seems I'll have to make my mama's famous fish casserole one Sunday and you'll see what you're missing," Jacob quipped, trying to keep things light and entertaining for his friend.

"Wait a second," Peter spoke up then between bites of food. "Are you saying that you, a fearsome sheriff, knows how to cook?"

"That's what makes me so fearsome, Peter," Jacob said trying for an air of confidence. "I'm always full of surprises." That got everyone laughing, and even a few maidens looked on with laughter.

"I'll have to see it to believe it," Peter retorted.

"Very well, then. I'll come out this Sunday and cook for you all," Jacob challenged, never really afraid to back down from a little good-hearted wager.

"I'll hold you to it, Sheriff," Peter said as he pointed his finger at Jacob before returning to his food.

"I think I shall come and visit Sunday as well to see what a fish casserole is," Brown Bear spoke up. "If it is good, then perhaps you'll teach it to the women of the tribe?" This got everyone laughing so loud that, at first, no one heard the cry of the baby. But Mathew was quick to shush them all as he quickly stood and listened. Clear as a bell, the cry of a baby was heard again and Jacob saw relief flood Mathew's face. Everyone stood and congratulated the new father then, slapping Mathew on the back or shaking his hand. Mathew was all smiles as he accepted all of their words of congratulations.

Jacob was quick to run to his horse and open up the saddle bag. He removed a small bottle of brandy he always kept on him in case of emergencies. He came back and offered everyone a drink in celebration to the newest Jenkins' addition.

"To Mathew and Jenny Jenkins," Jacob toasted before passing the bottle around. Mathew only took a small swig, not really keen to be drinking right before he met his newborn child. But it was worth seeing Brown Bear's reaction as he tasted the drink and coughed from the burn of the brandy.

"That is horrible," Brown Bear said as he coughed.

"You act like that's any worse than your fire water," Jacob retorted as he placed the cork back in the bottle and stuck it in the back pocket of his jeans.

"That is because it is," Brown Bear said as he stuck out his tongue. The action was so strange for the older Indian that Mathew couldn't help but laugh at the expression. Brown Bear crossed his arms over his bare chest, having only been wearing buck-skin trousers. But a large decorative necklace hung around his neck, signifying that the tall man with long black hair and almost black eyes was an Indian chief.

"I bet if you drank it more, you'd get used to it," Peter encouraged, but when Brown Bear gave the man a particularly stern look, the cattle hand quieted down again. Everyone's mirth bubbled over at the sight since they all knew that Peter could talk up a storm when given the chance. It was as they were all laughing and sharing in the comradery of the moment that the front door was opened.

Jacob watched Margret step out onto the front porch with a small bundle of cloth in her hands. She smiled sweetly at her son-in-law as she approached him with his newborn. She helped Mathew take the sleeping babe into his arms as Mathew stared down at the small baby with wide eyes.

"I'd like you to meet your new son," Margret said as she rested her hand on his shoulder.

"A boy? I have a son?" Mathew said in a soft voice as he looked from Margret to the baby.

"You sure do," Margret assured. She then looked around to see that several others had gathered since Mathew had first been sent to wait on the front porch. She smiled at them all, happy to be a grandmother at last.

"What are you going to name him, Boss?" Bobby spoke up then. Peter slapped his friend on the shoulder. "Hey, why'd you do that?"

"It's not like naming a pet, Bobby. Takes a good minute to name a child," Peter scolded.

"I think I like Michael for a name," Mathew answered, shifting his gaze to his cattle hands before looking down again on his son. "I suppose I should go in and see if Jenny likes the name."

"I know she'd enjoy getting to see you two together," Margret encouraged as she led them all back inside. When the door was closed, Jacob figured it was time to head back into town. Mother and father would be spending the rest of the night with their newborn, and thankfully Margret and Dr. Harvey were there to guide the new parents.

"Well, have a good night, fellas," Jacob said as he stepped off the porch and made his way towards his horse. "And thanks for the food, ladies." The maidens giggled as they started to collect their baskets and returned to their ponies in preparation for making their way back to camp. Peter and Bobby waved goodbye before making their way over to the bunkhouse. It had been constructed once they'd signed on as cattle hands at the ranch, and though it was a humble structure, it was enough for the two of them.

Jacob mounted his horse and tipped his hat to Brown Bear, then turned towards town and set his horse off into a gallop. It was late and he was eager to return home since the morning waited for no man. Though things had been quiet in Bear Creek, even with the mine being re-opened and all sorts of new miners coming into town, Jacob wasn't going to slack at his job just when he thought things were starting to cool down. He knew that with an increase of new people in town, that also meant that something terrible could be lurking just right around the corner.

Jacob's mind was full of thoughts as he rode into the night. Thankfully, town wasn't that far from the Jenkins' ranch and the night held a full moon to guide him all the way home. It allowed his mind to wander as he thought about Mathew and remembered how he and Jenny had fallen madly in love..

Jacob had to give Jenny credit where credit was due because she'd been through a lot before coming to Bear Creek. And when she did start to get settled out here in Montana, she sustained a nasty injury when she was out at the Indian camp with Mathew and the miners attacked the camp. Jacob shivered as he remembered being woken in the middle of the night to the news of the attack and having to come out into the forest to see so many dead. Now, her and Mathew's relationship was stronger than ever, and getting to be present during the birth of their son really showed Jacob just how much he wanted that type of happiness for himself.

Even with the re-opening of the mine, it only increased Bear Creek's biggest problem – a lack of marriageable women. Most men either needed to travel to meet women, or place a mail-order-bride ad themselves.

As Jacob made it back into town, he left his horse in the livery stables and walked through town to his own apartment above the Sheriff's Office. The town was quiet, just the way he liked it. In the morning, it would come alive again as the miners left the inn or the boarding house and made their way into the hills to do their work for the day. The town had greatly benefited from the mine being opened again and actually producing nuggets of gold and silver. Now Jacob only hoped that peace would remain in town and no one would try to start any trouble.

Letting out a deep sigh, Jacob pulled out his keys and unlocked the door. Once inside, he looked around the office then made his way up the stairs to the apartment. And even though he really wanted to just plop into bed and pass out, the wish to write his own mail-order-bride ad motivated him instead to sit down at his desk and pull out a sheet of writing paper. In the morning he would take it to Fry's and have it telegrammed to the newspapers in the East.

After Jacob had written the ad, he looked down at it, re-read it a few times, and then decided to start over. He never knew that writing three lines would be so difficult. He knew what he wanted in a wife, but as he looked down at the words, he wasn't sure if he was conveying his thoughts clearly enough. As he re-wrote it for a second time, then a third, he figured he'd come as close as he would to writing the perfect ad for himself.

Once the task was completed, Jacob blew out the lantern on his desk and made his way to his bed, stripping quickly out of his clothes and down to his long-johns. And after hanging up his hat on its hook, he finally rolled into bed and quickly found slumber after the long night. His last thought was him deciding that Mathew was the luckiest man in the world tonight and he hoped the new family would be able to rest as well.

CHAPTER 2

A few weeks had passed since little Michael had made his big appearance into the world. Margret often came to town to let the locals know how the new parents were doing. Jacob had even taken the time to order lunch for him and her at the inn during one of the days she was there doing housekeeping work just so he could hear how they were doing. Jacob had only been out to the ranch once. That was on a Sunday to cook the promised fish casserole, and to everyone's approval, Jacob had made the dish perfectly. Even Bobby agreed that it tasted quite good, but Brown Bear wasn't completely convinced that he'd like the dish again. Pasta was still a new concept to him, and though he'd eaten his plate clean, he said that he would postpone Jacob's lessons to the maidens in the art of cooking the dish.

When he could, Jacob got the latest details about the Jenkins from Margret, who continued to reassure everyone that Mathew and Jenny were doing fine, and that Michael was a happy little baby. It would be a while before Jenny felt up to returning to her cleaning duties and would probably remain home with the baby for some time, but many folks in town sent dinner and treats home with Margret as a way to send them joy and comfort. That was one of the best things about Bear Creek. Everyone was always willing to work together in order to support each other. Many were excited to know another generation of Jenkins had been born and would be raised up in the area.

And though Jacob had been doing his best to keep up on the latest around town, what he was really waiting for was letters to come in from the East in response to his mail-order-bride ad. He'd received a few already, asking what it was like being a sheriff and what exciting things he'd done while in the position. It wasn't exactly what he'd been expecting, thinking the authors of the letters would describe themselves rather than just wanting to learn more about him. He was hoping that whomever he agreed to have come to Bear Creek would be eager to get to know him for who he was and not what he did for a living. And, so far, the women who had written him had been more focused on marrying a sheriff then getting to know the real man behind the badge.

"Good morning, Sheriff," Tanner Williams said as he came into the Sheriff's Office. Tanner was Jacob's only deputy, and, so far, the young man had really proven himself. After the fiasco last year between the miners and the Indians, he made sure to keep Tanner well trained and ready for anything. Some evenings, they rode out of town and did a bit of target practice just to make sure they could take down criminals from a distance. Tanner had come into the office that morning just as Jacob was throwing away his latest letters.

"Morning, Tanner," Jacob replied as he stood and went over to the small wood stove that had a flat top large enough for him to boil some water and make a decent pot of coffee in the morning. He filled up his tin cup before returning to his desk once more.

"Seems like no luck yet," Tanner said as he gestured to the full trash bin. "Sure you don't want me to look over them for you just in case you might be missing out on the real deal?"

"No thank you, Tanner," Jacob said as he took a long sip of his coffee. "That would be an invasion of privacy. After all, no one said I had to reply to each one." Jacob was feeling frustrated that he hadn't received a decent letter yet. Only Tanner knew that he'd even placed an ad since his deputy had walked in on him plenty of times reading letters. He knew that he could trust him with what he was up to and he'd let everyone else know when he'd finally written a reply to a woman that interested him.

"Well, we should get going before we're late," Tanner said as he poured himself a small tin of coffee, quickly drank it all down, and set the cup back on his desk.

"What do you mean?" Jacob asked, trying to remember if they had a previous engagement.

"Edward James asked us to come out and check on his mining operation. He talked to you last week about wanting to keep things civil and figured if the Sheriff could put his stamp of approval on everything that the town wouldn't be so worried about another confrontation," Tanner explained as he placed his hands on his hips. It wasn't until Tanner spoke that Jacob began to remember his brief talk with Edward last week.

"It's a good thing you have a steel trap for a mind, Tanner," Jacob said as he finished his coffee and stood from his desk. After pulling on his hat, he followed Tanner out of the office before locking up and heading over to the livery stables. Jacob and Tanner said hello to all they passed on the way. Dan Mavis was calling all the school children to the town hall at that time. The building seconded as a church as well when Pastor Barthelme Munster was in town to give a sermon. It was also a decent place to gather when the town needed to make any big decisions. In the town hall was also a small office that Mayor Demetri Franklin used. He was continuously thinking of new ways to bring businesses and people, including women, to Bear Creek.

Once they were both saddled, Jacob and Tanner took a trail headed west from town through the forest. Slowly, the elevation began to rise as their horses rode higher and higher into the mountains. The trail from town was a bunch of switch-backs before plateauing into the heights of the mountains. If he took one of the trails to his right, Jacob would end up in the Indian camp. But today he took the one to the left to take him to the mines.

"Never ceases to amaze me how different everything is here in the forest," Tanner said as they traveled along the creek that the town was named after. Bears frequented the forest, and, more commonly, the creek to fish. Jacob was keeping his eyes peeled for any signs of bear since it was the springtime and bears would be more active in the area.

"I like being able to see what's coming," Jacob responded. "The wide-open plains surrounding town give me ample room to see people coming in from out of town. There are too many disadvantages in the forest." Tanner chuckled in response to his words as he shook his head, his sandy blond hair moving as he did so.

"There is more to life than just tactile advantages, Jacob," Tanner said as they crossed the creek and continued northwest through the mountains.

"When you're on the job, this is the way you should be thinking, Tanner. You never know what is right around the corner," Jacob said as he looked over his shoulder at Tanner. But as he looked at his deputy, he saw that the color had drained out of his face as he raised a shaky finger and pointed directly in front of Jacob. The Sheriff's instincts kicked in as he spun around in his saddle to see what was directly ahead of them.

Jacob's eyes went wide as he spotted a momma bear with her cubs. The bear was a few yards in front of them, having just stepped out from behind a thicket of trees with her little ones behind her. But as soon as the bear spotted the two horses, she immediately rocked back on her feet and stood to her full height, making Jacob swallow hard as he took in the large bear.

"Just lead the horses backwards slowly," Jacob said in a soft voice, trying not to even move his lips. Any sudden movement could cause the animal to charge, and neither one of them was prepared for a real fight against a bear. Jacob pulled on the reins, signaling for his horse to stop, when the bear let out a terrible growl that shook the air. Jacob's horse reared up, throwing Jacob to the ground, where he landed on a cluster of boulders and trees. He screamed out as he landed hard on his right arm, agonizing pain shooting through his arm and shoulder to the point where his vision started to become fuzzy and black.

Jacob heard several gun shots. He was in such a haze of pain that he couldn't even focus on what was happening around him. He tried to get up from where he'd fallen, but the slightest movement caused the pain to increase. He forced his eyes open, knowing that the bear could come after him if he was injured and not running away.

Tanner was running towards him after unloading his gun and scaring the bear and her cubs away. All Tanner was concerned about was making sure his boss was okay. But as he came to Jacob's side and saw the amount of blood that was coming from his arm, Tanner knew that the Sheriff was in serious trouble.

"Hold on, Jacob. I'll get you to Dr. Harvey and he'll fix you right up," Tanner said as he pulled Jacob to his feet. Jacob cried out in pain, letting loose a string of cuss words as he tried to gain his balance. His knees wobbled together and he knew he wasn't going to remain standing for long. He fell to his knees then, using his good arm to stop him from falling over completely.

"Take your horse and ride over to the Indian camp. Tell Brown Bear what has happened," Jacob ordered as he sat down on the ground and tried to remain conscious amongst all the pain. "His people have a doctor of sorts and will be able to help get me back into town."

"But what about the bear?" Tanner asked, his face riddled with panic.

"Tanner, get going so you can get back and we won't have to worry about it," Jacob said, his voice growing stern as he used his good arm to shove Tanner away from him. "Now get going." Tanner stumbled back and quickly mounted his horse, digging his heels into the beast to have him galloping across the mountains to the Indian camp. Jacob did his best to remain conscious just long enough to see Tanner disappear around the bend before he slumped onto his back and completely passed out from the pain.

WHEN JACOB WAS ROUSED AGAIN, his head was foggy as he forced himself to open his eyes. He'd been expecting to feel the hard ground beneath him from where he'd lost consciousness, but instead he felt warmth and cushions all around him. Jacob turned his head slowly and spied Dr. Harvey sitting in a chair beside him with Brown Bear and a few of his Indian braves standing in the back of the room. Jacob was confused and disoriented and was about to fall asleep once more when Dr. Harvey moved smelling salts underneath his nose to wake him back up again.

"Rise and shine, sonny. I need to make sure your arm is set properly," Dr. Harvey said as Jacob came to. He groaned, the lantern hanging from the ceiling causing him to cringe against the light. Several other candles burned in the room and as Jacob's eyes adjusted, he realized that he was resting in the clinic in town.

"What happened, Doc?" Jacob asked as he allowed the doctor to roll him onto his left side so he could move and manipulate Jacob's arm. The pain quickly returned and he was sure he was going to pass out once more.

"Stay with me, Jacob. Your arm needs bandaging and put in a plaster cast and I need your help for that," Dr. Harvey said in a stern voice. Jacob did his best to stay awake but was losing the battle and it wasn't until Brown Bear came forward and began to tickle the bottoms of his feet that he came wide awake.

"Hey, stop that!" Jacob hollered, thinking that now was not the time for such games.

"If it helps you stay awake, then I shall continue," Brown Bear said. "My old friend, I am concerned for your safety. When Tanner ran into our camp and explained what had happened, I was sure that if you were left unprotected, you would be attacked by any bears in the area. I raced back to the spot with Tanner and a few of my Indian braves. Do you know I spotted a bear on the other side of the clearing, deciding if it could make you its next meal?"

Then Brown Bear told Jacob that all of them together had carried Jacob back to town in a woven carrier from their camp. "I could see how badly your right arm was damaged. Now I want to do whatever it takes to make sure you, my friend, survive and recover without delay. Therefore, I shall tickle your bare feet while Dr. Harvey does what is needed."

There was a loud popping sound as Dr. Harvey relocated Jacob's arm once more. Jacob cried out in agony, starting to shake as the pain coursed through him. He felt terribly cold all of a sudden and wasn't sure what was happening to him.

"Just a bit more," Dr. Harvey said in a strained voice as he began to move Jacob's arm around till it was properly in place before he began to wrap it and place splints all up and down his arm. Even with Brown Bear tickling the bottoms of his feet, Jacob was quickly falling asleep, needing to hide from all the pain.

"Alright, that should do it for now," Dr. Harvey said. "I'll mix together the casting materials and then wrap the arm in plaster so it won't be able to move till it's healed."

"Will I ever be able to use my right arm again?" Jacob asked in a strained voice. He was terrified of losing his ability to shoot a pistol and protect the people of Bear Creek. He wouldn't be able to remain a sheriff if that happened.

"For now, Jacob, rest. Here, I've prepared some laudanum for you to help with the pain," Dr. Harvey said as he moved to a side table while Jacob tried his best to remain breathing and unmoving. Dr. Harvey returned to his side and helped him drink a spoon-full of the medicine that tasted bitter. But a few minutes later, the room faded to darkness and he was able to sleep soundly.

CHAPTER 3

*R*osa Casey hurried up the servant's stairs to the second floor of the Boston, Massachusetts manor where she was employed as a lady's maid for Miss Katelyn Trevino. Her madam was Boston's most popular debutante, and since Miss Trevino had a very important tea party to attend, or at least that is what she'd exclaimed the night before, Rosa wanted to make sure her charge was up early and prepared for the said event.

Rosa could hear the spring birds chirping happily as she opened up the servant's door that allowed her main access to the second floor. She closed it quietly behind her, unsure if the master and mistress of the house were awake yet. They'd attended a ball the night before and would no doubt be sleeping right through the morning. Miss Trevino had been displeased about not being able to attend because it was meant for married couples only, and therefore had talked all night with Rosa about her plans for the next day and the gentlemen she was hoping to impress at the evening's dinner party.

It had been almost ten years since Rosa, twelve-years-old, had been brought from the orphanage to the Trevino estate. She'd been classically trained by Mrs. Trevino's very experienced lady's maid to look after Katelyn, the Trevino's ten-year-old daughter. In essence,

Rosa and Katelyn had grown up together with Rosa making sure that Katelyn's every need was taken care of. In return, Katelyn treated Rosa as more of a friend than a servant to order around. Since Rosa had learned that Mrs. Trevino did not share the same opinion as her daughter when it came to how to treat the staff, Rosa was grateful to be Katelyn's lady's maid instead of her mother's.

Rosa opened the door to Katelyn's room and shut it behind her before going over to the window and drawing open the curtains. Morning sunlight poured into the room, forcing Katelyn to roll over in her bed to try to hide from it. Rosa smirked, knowing that it was a sure way to get Katelyn to wake up. Rosa then began drawing a bath for her charge in the water closet, knowing how Katelyn liked a nice warm bath first thing in the morning as a way to prepare for important social events.

"Rise and shine, Miss Trevino," Rosa said in a sing-song voice. She stopped for a moment in front of the looking glass and made sure that her golden curls were still tucked back behind her head. She couldn't help that she'd been born with curly hair when Mrs. Trevino liked all the maids to wear their hair up in a bun. It was a little difficult for Rosa to do so, but she'd been trying to perfect the look since she was twelve. Now that she was twenty-two, Rosa liked to think that hairstyles were the least of her worries.

"Come on, Katelyn. You don't want to be late for the tea party this morning," Rosa urged as she went to Katelyn's wardrobe and pulled open the doors, looking through her many gowns to see which one would be perfect for the occasion.

"I don't understand how you can be so happy in the mornings," Katelyn said as she eventually sat up in bed and rubbed the sleep from her eyes. Her long, black hair flowed down her back in waves. Katelyn wasn't only popular, she was beautiful as well. It was probably one of the many reasons why she was an up-and-coming debutante. And though Rosa liked to think of herself as attractive as well, she'd never be able to compete with a young lady such as Katelyn.

"I'm happy because I have no reason not to be," Rosa reasoned as she pulled a gown from the wardrobe and set it on the hook by the changing area in the bedroom. As Katelyn got up from the bed and went into the water closet to take care of her business, Rosa made the bed and fluffed the pillows just the way she knew Katelyn liked them.

One of the other maids came into the room then carrying the morning tea tray and light breakfast. Since Katelyn would be attending a brunch get-together with other ladies of society, she knew that her madam wouldn't be wanting to have a very large breakfast. So, she'd had a few pieces of toast and jam prepared for her. After dismissing the maid, Rosa made up Katelyn's morning cup of tea herself, always enjoying making the simple drink. Katelyn often complimented Rosa for her skills at making the absolute perfect cup of tea, so she always took great pleasure in doing so every morning.

"My goodness, what a wonderful morning," Katelyn said with a heavy sigh as she emerged freshly bathed. Rosa chuckled, knowing how Katelyn always had a better temper after she'd taken her morning bath. Rosa followed Katelyn over to the room's changing area as she towel-dried her skin before helping her into her undergarments and finally the gown she'd picked out for her.

"Great taste as normal, Rosa dear," Katelyn said as she turned back and forth before the looking glass, taking in her reflection and appearance.

"Thank you," Rosa replied as she had Katelyn sit before the mirror with her cup of tea as she started to dry her hair with the towel and brush it out before pinning the tresses up into one of the latest styles. It was Rosa's job to make sure she was current with all the trends of Boston to ensure that Katelyn always looked her best and appeared to be knowledgeable of fashion. Katelyn taught her much of what it was like to live as a lady, and if Rosa had been born into a prestigious family instead of being left at the orphanage, she was convinced that they'd attend every social gathering together.

A long time ago, Rosa stopped dreaming about herself in Katelyn's shoes. She was happy to have a good paying position within the house of such a prestigious family. Compared to other lady's maids that she'd met in the past, Rosa knew that she had a pretty good life. Her charge was kind and compassionate, and her salary was desirable.

Therefore, she had no reason to want to change to another household or imagine her life in a way that it wasn't. Nonetheless, Rosa still longed for a better life for herself. After all, she did want to marry one day.

"What are you thinking about, Rosa?" Katelyn asked, noticing the way that Rosa was getting lost in her thoughts as she teased her hair into a cushion arrangement on the top of her head, secured with tortoiseshell combs, with a carefully artless selection of tresses falling either side of her face.

"Oh, nothing very important," Rosa said as she looked at Katelyn through the looking glass, surprised that Katelyn noticed her daydreaming. She smiled at Katelyn as she asked, "Tell me again about this tea party. Who all will be there?"

Rosa knew how to easily distract her charge as Katelyn began to happily chatter about all the other young ladies who would be attending the brunch. To Katelyn, it was very important for her to keep up social appearances. Even more so around ladies of her class and status in society. It was her way of sizing up her competition when it came to winning over the hearts of the most eligible gentlemen in the city. Rosa found it all very amusing to listen to Katelyn talk about things that were rather trivial to her. But the idea of marrying was something that Rosa was fond of and was a bit jealous of Katelyn for her ability to choose whomever she wished to marry while Rosa rarely had the time to meet eligible men.

Rosa never dreamed of meeting a wealthy gentleman like Katelyn often described, but she liked the idea of meeting a family man, someone who worked hard for a living and wanted a large family like she did. Since she'd been raised as an orphan, a sense of family was something that Rosa was still learning about. One day she wanted to fall in love and marry the man of her dreams while also planning on having a family with at least four or five children. Rosa smiled at the idea because she was already excited at the thought of having children and raising them in a loving home.

"Rosa, you are doing it again," Katelyn said once she realized her lady's maid, and perhaps her closest friend, was no longer listening to her talk about the brunch. "What are you really thinking about, and don't fib this time." Rosa sighed as she lowered her hands from Katelyn's hair. She looked at her charge and figured that sharing her thoughts wouldn't hurt.

"I was just thinking about what it would be like to fall in love and marry a wonderful man. Then, the thought of having a large family one day," Rosa said simply. A bright smile crept onto Katelyn's face as she turned in the chair to face her.

"I know you will, Rosa. Once I have married and moved to my new home, I'm sure you'd be free to marry whomever. After all, you won't have a position here anymore," Katelyn said in a happy tone. Rosa chuckled, knowing that Katelyn had little sense of how people in lower classes courted one another.

"It is a bit hard to find someone of my status to marry," Rosa confessed as she turned from Katelyn and brought over the plate of toast. Katelyn accepted it as she also took Rosa's hand in hers, forcing Rosa to look into the beautiful brown eyes of her charge.

"Rosa, never place yourself so low that you settle for less than you deserve," Katelyn urged before letting go of her hand. "And if you can't find someone suitable in Boston, then why don't you become a mail-order-bride?" Rosa chuckled again as she went to the task of taking care of Katelyn's laundry.

"How can anyone fall in love through letters?" Rosa pondered out loud. "What if I do decide to write someone and I arrive in the West with my dear Sheba to only find out that the gentleman is a complete snob who had lied during our correspondence."

Katelyn giggled as she put down her plate of toast and went over to the table by the door where the morning paper had been delivered. She opened it up and started to flip through the pages till she arrived at the *Matrimonial Times*. Then, she folded back the paper before handing it to Rosa. Katelyn then returned to her chair as she began to nibble on her toast.

"You never know what will happen until you take a chance," Katelyn said between bites. "If you reply to one of these ads and decide to go out West to meet the man, I will not only pay for your ticket and all of the things you'll need, but I will pay for your return ticket as well for you and Sheba if anything disastrous were to happen." Rosa looked up from the paper at Katelyn, surprised by such a generous offer. Though Katelyn often gifted Rosa things she no longer wanted or received from suitors she did not care about, this was a much more generous offer..

"You certainly can't be serious," Rosa said. "Why on earth would you give me so much?"

"Rosa, you've been my only friend these many years you've been my lady's maid. You're practically like my sister. Therefore, you should know how much I care about you and want to see you happily married one day."

Rosa looked back down at the paper and started to read through some of the ads. "Wyoming rancher seeks a slim woman who can keep house," she read. "My goodness, that sounds dreadful."

"But you do have the desired skills," Katelyn offered. "You're tall, beautifully blonde, have mesmerizing deep brown eyes with a figure any man would like to squeeze." Rosa couldn't contain her laughter at being described so. She looked back at the paper and read some more of the ads.

"Rancher, rancher, miner, bounty hunter?" Rosa said as she glanced at Katelyn, who seemed to be fighting off a fit of giggles as she listened to Rosa read out loud. "These all sound ridiculous." But as Rosa went on to the next ad, she had to admit that one had caught her attention.

"What is it, Rosa?" Katelyn asked. Rosa looked up at her for a moment before wetting her lips and reading out loud:.

"Sheriff Jacob Benning of Bear Creek, Montana is in search of a family oriented young woman with skills that could add to the remote town. Bear Creek is a miner's town with very few eligible women. I'm hoping to meet a woman who will love me for who I am and not grow too worried about my position in town."

"Well, well. A sheriff? Now that sounds exciting," Katelyn reasoned. "He's family oriented and seems to really care about his town if he's willing to describe it in his ad."

"Yes, I think that is what caught my eye," Rosa admitted. "He's not just describing what he wants or what makes him an ideal husband. This sheriff really seems to care about his town."

"Bear Creek, Montana," Katelyn said slowly, seeming to test saying the name of the town to see if she liked it. Rosa knew she did the same thing with French cuisine and couldn't help but chuckle as she folded up the newspaper and set it aside.

"Well, that is enough of that. I'm going to go take care of the laundry," Rosa said as she collected her charge's laundry once more into her arms.

"Please tell me you'll write to this sheriff if only to satisfy my curiosity," Katelyn urged as Rosa went to leave the room. She stopped and took a deep breath before turning around to face her charge.

"I promise I will do so this evening when I have a spare moment," Rosa promised. "Now, I'm going to let Roberts know you are ready for the day and to have the carriage prepared for you."

"Thank you, Rosa," Katelyn called after her as she left the room and hurried down the hallway to the servant's door. Once through it, Rosa felt like she could breathe easier. She wasn't keen on the idea of writing the sheriff with the idea of becoming a mail-order-bride. She'd never left Boston before and wasn't sure if she could really do it now. And though she had all the domestic skills that a husband might desire in a wife, she still had to decide if she'd be willing to go through with it.

After Rosa had finished with the laundry, she found another copy of the morning's newspaper in the servant's room and took it with her lunch to her room. There, she was greeted by her tabby-cat, Sheba, whom she'd rescued from outside when a terrible thunderstorm had hit Boston. Mr. Trevino had given Rosa permission to keep the cat in her room as long as the animal didn't get out or stink up the servant's quarters. And since Rosa left open her window just wide enough for the cat to come and go, she didn't have to worry too much. As long as Rosa had food for Sheba, the cat always returned to her.

"Hello, my dear," Rosa greeted the cat as she came into her room and shut the door. She took her lunch to her writing desk and set it there as she got settled on the chair. Her room was rather small compared to Katelyn's, but Rosa had never had reason to complain. Since it was just her and Sheba, Rosa didn't need all that much room. And since Mrs. Trevino required all the maids to wear a uniform, she had very little clothing besides what she needed for work.

Sheba came and rubbed herself against Rosa's leg, wanting attention and, no doubt, some of her lunch. She tore a piece of chilled sandwich meat from her plate and gave it to the cat, who happily took it and ran to the other side of the room to enjoy her treat. Rosa cared about Sheba even though she was still very much a wild cat. The idea of having to transport her from Massachusetts all the way to Montana didn't sit well with her. But first, Rosa reminded herself, she would need to write the Sheriff to see if things would even work out between them.

Rosa turned her attention to her letter then, as she pulled out a sheet of writing paper and prepared her quill in the ink. After taking a bite of her sandwich, she then began to construct her letter to the Sherriff.

Dear Jacob Benning,

My charge challenged me today to write to you, and since I am always willing to please my lady, I accepted her challenge after we both agreed that your ad was the only reasonable one in the entire paper. I will not go into detail on what made the other ads so distasteful but you should feel proud in knowing that you were chosen out of the whole lot of them.

My name is Rosa Casey and I'm a lady's maid for the Trevino family here in Boston. This family is one of the most prestigious in the city, so I am proud of my position and whom I get to work for. Since I am an orphan, it's been nice to stay with this family since I was twelve and feel a part of the entire household.

My lady will soon marry, I have no doubt in that. She's a very popular debutante and has almost every eligible gentleman in Boston after her hand in marriage. And once she is married, I will be left without a charge. Therefore, I too have turned my thoughts to the idea of marriage since I've always wanted to be part of a large family.

While I'm sure of myself as a suitable wife, there are not many eligible gentlemen in this city who catch my interest. I want to meet a man whom I can fall in love with, who I can respect as a hard worker, and more importantly, who will make an excellent father for our children. One of the things I was able to deduce from your ad is that you care a lot about your town because you took the time to mention it in your ad. This shows me that you're a caring person and also have a great respect for your position within your community.

My lady has promised that if I do decide to come out West that she will pay for the entire trip. She's always been very generous, and I do take her word for truth. So, I feel that I have no reason not to try to be a mail-order-bride. I am ready to begin a new life as a wife and mother and hope to meet a man I can fall in love with. I have no children of my own from any previous relationship, but I do have a tabby-cat that I rescued, named Sheba. I don't know if you like pets, but I thought that honesty is the best policy.

I look forward to your reply letter and hope you'll describe to me what Bear Creek is like.

Rosa Casey

JACOB WAS TRYING to concentrate on writing up a report on a miner that Edward had to fire when he caught the man stealing equipment at night. When Edward had dragged the man in, hog-tied and everything, Jacob knew that Edward James was a man to reckon with. But the most frustrating part of the report that would have normally taken him a few minutes to complete had now taken him two hours. With his right arm still in a cast and pinned to his body with a sling, Jacob had been forced to right the report with his left hand.

Jacob grumbled to himself as Tanner came into the Sheriff's Office. Jacob didn't even bother looking up as Tanner set a stack of mail on his desk and then shuffled off to his own. It was no secret that Jacob had become a little rough around the edges ever since his accident. Normal things that Jacob never really paid attention to were now the most tedious of tasks for him. Getting dressed in the morning, cooking for himself, and even taking care of the calls of nature had all become difficult. And if he even bumped his arm just a little bit, hot pain would shoot up his arm, into his shoulder, and down his back.

"Tanner, I'm going to need you to write this report," Jacob said as he looked up at Tanner. He was sitting at his desk and looking at Jacob, waiting for the Sheriff to see that he had more mail. Jacob squinted his eyes at his deputy, trying to figure out what he was doing. He then glanced down at his desk and saw the many letters that were addressed to him.

"I don't have time to be reading any letters," Jacob grumbled as he held up the report for Tanner to take. The deputy stood and took the report and settled back down at his desk.

"With me doing all the work around here, seems like you got all the time in the world," Tanner quipped as he withdrew his writing quill and ink pot from within his dresser drawer. Jacob looked at him for a moment, wanting to stare a hole in him. But as Tanner got to work on the report, Jacob figured he had nothing to lose at this point.

Opening the letters with one hand was another tedious task. He tried to use the fingers from his right hand for help, but they proved to be of little use when they could barely move without causing him pain. Eventually, he got the first of the letters opened and began to read it. After a few minutes, he used his left hand to crumple up the letter and throw it into the waste basket before moving on to the next one. With his poor attitude, Jacob was probably a little harder on judging each letter. It wasn't until he came upon a particular one from Boston that he really paid attention.

As Jacob leaned forward on his desk and started to read the letter slowly, he chuckled to himself after reading the opening paragraph. It was comical that this author had compared his ad to others and had determined his to be the most compelling. And the fact that her charge had urged her to write was another interesting part of this letter. The more Jacob read, the more he liked the fact that she'd written more about herself than asking him multiple questions about his job.

Tanner had stopped working on the report when he noticed how engulfed Jacob had become in the letter in his hands. He'd never seen him this interested in any letter before and had just accepted the fact that the Sheriff would more than likely toss all the letters he was receiving till his arm healed and he was back to being his normal self. But as Tanner watched Jacob's facial expressions as they changed from surprise, to humor, to complete concentration, the deputy couldn't help but hope that this could finally be the one.

After Jacob read and re-read the letter, he knew that he wanted to reply to this Rosa Casey. He found her intriguing and liked that she was both comical but knew what she wanted in life. Jacob wasn't so sure about her cat since he'd never really cared for felines, but if he ended up falling in love with Rosa, he'd be willing to like her cat as well. The only problem he currently faced now was writing a reply letter to Rosa. As he looked down at his casted right arm, he knew that it was going to be a terribly difficult task.

Jacob slowly took out a sheet of writing paper and prepared his quill. He held it steady in his left hand as he thought about what he wanted to write before he set about doing so. The last thing he wanted was to begin and decide to scrap the whole sheet of paper. She'd written about her life in Boston, what she did for work, and all her hopes and dreams in just a few short lines. Jacob could tell the young woman was intelligent even if she did work as a lady's maid. He wanted to portray the same in his letter but knew that his handwriting would have to be clear enough first.

Just as he went to write his first sentences, figuring he'd make the letter short and straight to the point, Tanner spoke up and broke his concentration.

"Want me to write that for you?" Tanner asked as Jacob's left hand went wide with the quill, causing him to mess up his first word. Jacob ground his teeth together as he looked up at his deputy. He was doing his best to control his temper as he crumpled up the piece of paper, not liking the idea of starting over when writing paper wasn't exactly easy to come by in Bear Creek.

"No, Tanner. I don't want you to write for me because that would be an invasion of privacy," Jacob explained as he pulled out another sheet of writing paper and went to go wet his quill once more when Tanner spoke again.

"But you want the young lady to be able to read your letter and not think you're illiterate," Tanner reasoned as he went to stand up and come over to him, but Jacob raised his left hand and pointed his quill at him, stopping Tanner from moving.

"I must do this on my own, Tanner," Jacob said. "It wouldn't be fair if I asked you to help because you'd need to read her letter and also know my personal thoughts." Tanner sighed as he finished standing all the way.

"In that case, I'm going to go send this telegram and leave you with some time to write your letter then," Tanner said as he picked up the report off his desk and moved to the door. He dipped his head towards Jacob, and he returned the gesture, grateful for a moment alone to get this done.

Now that Jacob had a moment alone, he went about drafting his letter to Rosa. Since his handwriting wasn't the best with his left hand he moved slowly, trying to write each letter as clearly as possible.

Dear Miss Rosa Casey,

Thank you for writing me. Forgive my poor handwriting. I recently broke my right arm after my horse was spooked by a bear and now I'm forced to write with my left hand. Your letter was very interesting to me and I enjoyed learning about you and your life in Boston. I feel that we have similar goals in life, to one day marry for love and have a decent sized family. I hope that we both accomplish what we want in life.

Bear Creek is a miner's town. It was first created when miners went into the nearby mountains for gold and silver. And now that the mine has been re-bought and has been successful as of late, Bear Creek is starting to boom once more. Yet, there are no single women here, so that is why I decided to place a mail-order-bride ad.

The thing I love most about Bear Creek is that everyone works together in this community. We might not have much, but we have enough to support one another and ensure that all our needs are met. I enjoy serving this community and making sure everyone is safe. With my deputy, Tanner Williams, we are able to do that.

There is a local Indian tribe right outside of town who reside in the mountains. I am friends with their Chief, Brown Bear, who is a considerate and just man. It is fun to banter with him from time to time and introduce him to civilized ways.

Well, I'm sure it's hard to read most of this and I've probably written more than I should. But I hope this letter gives you a better idea of me. I look forward to your reply,

Jacob Benning

AS JACOB LOOKED over his letter, he did his best not to grimace at it. He'd written from his heart, hoping to shed light on what it was like here in Bear Creek. Jacob wanted Rosa to understand all the most important parts: that it was a remote town contingent on the mine being successful, that there weren't many women here, and that there were Indians close by. He figured these were all important aspects of Bear Creek to note since she was used to living in a large city and probably had never encountered a miner or an Indian before.

Once the ink dried, Jacob reasoned that this letter was the best he was going to be able to produce till his arm healed. And since Dr. Harvey had explained that his arm wouldn't be fully healed until Christmas, Jacob knew that he had to be more patient with himself and not get frustrated so easily.

With a deep sigh, Jacob folded up the letter and addressed it. After putting on his hat, he took the letter and left the Sheriff's Office. He locked the door behind him, knowing he'd probably pass Tanner on his way to Fry's to post his letter and he could just give the keys to his deputy. With the mercantile only being a short walk from the Sheriff's Office, he wasn't too worried about stepping out for a moment. With the letter to Rosa in his hand, he had a little more hope than before that he'd one day meet a woman whom he could proudly call his wife.

CHAPTER 4

*R*osa was in the middle of pulling the laundry off the drying line in the way back yard beside the gardens when Mr. Bentley came out to her, holding a letter out her way. She smiled kindly at the butler as she set Miss Trevino's clothes into the basket and accepted the missive, quickly looking down to see who it was from.

"Thank you, Mr. Bentley, for coming out all this way to bring me my post," Rosa said as she looked back up at the older man with a bright smile. Excitement ran through her to see that it was from Jacob Benning, but now wasn't the time to open it. She was right in the middle of her workday and needed to get this laundry put away in Katelyn's room.

"You're welcome, Miss Casey. I know you don't ever receive letters, so I thought I'd specially deliver it to you myself," Mr. Bentley replied.

"That's very kind of you," Rosa said as she put the letter in her apron pocket and then returned to pulling the dry gowns and under-garments off the line and preparing to take them inside. She listened to Mr. Bentley's footsteps as he left. Just for a quick moment, Rosa took the letter out from her pocket and looked at it again if only to confirm she'd read the address correctly and that it was indeed written by Jacob. She giggled excitedly as she placed it back in her apron and picked up the large basket of dried clothes and carried them inside to fold and put away in Katelyn's room.

It wasn't until she reached the second floor of the manor that Rosa realized that she'd been happily humming to herself. She laughed at herself as she opened the servant's door, and checking to make sure the hallway was clear, she quickly made her way to Katelyn's room to finish her chore so she could read what Jacob had written her.

With Katelyn being out of the house, enjoying the afternoon shopping with her mother and close friends, Rosa didn't have to worry about her charge as she opened up the bedroom door and came in. She set the clean laundry down on the floor beside the wardrobe and proceeded to hang up her many gowns when Katelyn came running into the room, tears streaming down her face as she closed the door behind her.

"Katelyn, what on Earth is the matter?" Rosa asked as she came over to Katelyn and wrapped her arms around her shoulders, embracing her dear friend.

"I just read in the papers to see that my Fredrick has announced his engagement to another when he promised me just two nights ago that he'd soon ask my father permission to marry me," Katelyn explained through her sobs. Rosa rubbed her back, allowing her to cry into her shoulder. As her body shook with sobs, Rosa simply held her close and hummed softly to her. Rosa's heart was breaking for her dear friend because she knew how fond she was of Fredrick, who had already had some success as an inventor. But it now seemed that he was just playing with her heart the whole time.

"Alright, my dear. Let's get you out of your walking dress and into a bath. I'll pick out something more comfortable for you," Rosa said as she coaxed Katelyn down into a chair. She then hurried to start the bath before gathering some clean garments for Katelyn to wear afterwards. Once the water was ready, she helped Katelyn change out of her clothes and eased her down into the bath before leaving her for a moment to find a maid to bring up a tea tray for her charge.

After readying a new outfit and putting away the rest of the clean laundry, Rosa then went to go check on Katelyn to find tears still streaming down her face. Her heart dropped as she kneeled beside the tub and used a clean cloth to wash her face and hair. Rosa used the soap that Katelyn loved the most, taking her time to thoroughly clean her and wash out her hair before helping her out of the tub once the water began to cool.

"Perhaps I should become a mail-order-bride?" Katelyn wondered out loud as Rosa helped her into some fresh clothes. The gown she'd chosen was a simple day gown of a lilac color that would surely help Katelyn to feel better. But as Rosa listened to what Katelyn had said, she was growing worried that her charge might do something reckless with her broken heart.

"You are capable of marrying a fine man of great wealth and means," Rosa said, trying to remind Katelyn of her position in society. "And you would devastate your parents if you simply ran away."

"I like to think life is easier in the West," Katelyn said as she sat before the looking glass so Rosa could comb out her hair. "There would be no pressure from society, and no one would really care whom you chose to marry or anything."

"Oh, I'm sure that living in a frontier town comes with all its own hardships. I surely couldn't imagine you cooking or cleaning for yourself, let alone a family," Rosa said with a wink at Katelyn. "Can you really give up being waited on, everything done for you, choosing new gowns even if you don't need them? All for just a little more freedom?"

"What am I going to do, Rosa?" Katelyn asked as tears threatened to fall from her eyes again.

"You're going to continue on as you always have," Rosa said as she pulled the comb through her hair. "Tonight at the dinner party, you're going to act like nothing is wrong and you never really cared about Fredrick. Because after all, he was never going to be good enough for you. And then, once you've forgotten him, you'll then meet the man you were always meant to be with and you'll wonder why you ever shed a tear over that scum of the earth." Katelyn giggled while she listened to Rosa.

"You really think that I'll meet a man one day that will take care of me as good as you do?" Katelyn asked, hope shining in her eyes as she looked at Rosa through the looking glass.

"Keep your heart guarded and make a man work for it, and I promise you Katelyn that you'll find the one you were always destined for," Rosa advised as she looked back in the mirror at her dear friend. When Katelyn smiled at her, she was certain she'd finally said the right thing to bring up her spirits.

"Speaking of destiny, have you heard back from the Sheriff?" Katelyn asked, eager to know if any developments had been made between the two. Rosa sighed with a happy smile as she set the comb aside and pulled out the letter from Jacob, showing it to Katelyn through the mirror. Katelyn clapped excitedly as she turned around, giving Rosa her full attention.

"I just received it today and haven't had a moment to read it yet," Rosa explained as she took to a chair near her friend. "How about we do that right now?" Katelyn nodded excitedly as she folded her hands in her lap as though she was about to receive an enjoyable lesson from one of her favorite tutors. Rosa figured that in a way, she was like a teacher to Katelyn. While Katelyn had taught her all about living as an elite lady in society, Rosa liked to think that she'd taught Katelyn about the more important things in life like love and friendship.

As Rosa slowly opened up the letter, she was pleased to see that it was a good length as she noticed writing on both sides of the paper, but as she went to read the first sentence, her brows pressed together as she tried to decipher the words.

"My goodness, what poor handwriting," Rosa exclaimed as she turned it over and showed Katelyn. Her friend looked as confused as her as Rosa went back to trying to read the letter. "I would have never known a sheriff could write so poorly...." Rosa's voice trailed off as she made out the first two sentences, and as she understood the reason for his bad handwriting, Rosa couldn't help but chuckle a little.

"Oh, he writes that his horse was spooked by a bear and he was thrown from it, breaking his right arm in the process," Rosa explained to Katelyn. She gasped as she covered her mouth with her hand like a lady was supposed to.

"You're telling me that he lives where bears roam wildly?" Katelyn asked, shocked to hear about the horrible accident.

"Well, it must have been named Bear Creek for a reason," Rosa suggested. "My word, he certainly tried his best. He had to write this whole letter with his left hand."

"At least he tried," Katelyn offered. "I can't imagine riding a horse or being thrown from it."

"I've only ridden a horse once or twice, but I guess when you live in a remote town, you have to get around somehow," Rosa said. She then fell silent as she studied the rest of the letter, reading it slowly to both understand the words but also to take in everything Jacob had written to her about. She liked learning about Bear Creek and tried to envision herself there. She wasn't so certain about meeting Indians, but if Jacob was good friends with an Indian chief, perhaps it wouldn't be all that bad. Rosa was also concerned about the fact that there weren't many women in Bear Creek. Did that mean she wouldn't really have an opportunity to make new friends?

"I can't tell what your reaction is to his letter," Katelyn admitted as Rosa folded up the letter and placed it in her apron pocket. Rosa met Katelyn's eyes and tried to smile for her friend.

"I think Jacob possesses a good bit of humor," Rosa said, wanting to stay positive and not focus so much on her concerns about Bear Creek. "I like how he talks about Bear Creek and the sense of community there. And he's very realistic in his letter. He isn't trying to hide anything."

"But?" Katelyn urged, wanting to know how her friend truly felt about the letter.

"Sometimes I get concerned over whether or not I'll be happy in Bear Creek," Rosa said. "I like the idea of traveling out West just to see what it is like or meeting a man I can fall in love with. But what if I don't like it there? What if I make no friends because Jacob explains there are not many women there but primarily miners and the townspeople? I just don't know." Rosa looked down at her fingers, knowing she was being quite cowardly right now, but she couldn't deny how she was honestly feeling.

Katelyn reached out and took her friend's hand,. "And all of these things you won't know until you go," Katelyn reminded her. "It won't hurt to reply to the Sheriff and see where these letters lead you both. Instead of thinking of what can go wrong, think about what could possibly go right." Rosa smiled then as she looked back up at her friend, nodding because she knew that Katelyn was right. It seemed that today they had good advice for each other when it came to matters of the heart.

"Now, I must get some rest. All this crying has worn me out and I want to be my best before this dinner party tonight," Katelyn said as she rose from the chair and approached her bed. "I'll need help with my hair and gown around 4 o'clock."

"Of course," Rosa said as she rose from the chair, remembering her place. Though her and Katelyn were close friends, she still had a job to do. "I'll have a tea tray ready for you when you wake." Rosa curtsied and left the room, wanting to write Jacob back as soon as she could. After talking with the maid to bring back up the tea tray at 4 o'clock, Rosa made her way back downstairs through the servant's staircase, wanting to take a minute to construct her letter.

As Rosa made her way to her small room, she opened the door and closed it behind her quickly so Sheba couldn't make her way into the main house. She hadn't allowed her cat to escape yet and she wasn't going to risk the incident ever being able to take place. But as Rosa looked around her room and under her bed, she saw that the tabby-cat wasn't even in her room and must have gone out through the window.

Unconcerned, Rosa sat down at her writing desk and withdrew a sheet of writing paper before preparing her quill. She thought about her response for a moment and then began to write her reply to Jacob, smiling as she imagined watching him writing the letter with his left hand.

~

On a Saturday afternoon, Jacob was practicing mounting and dismounting his horse in the corral outside the livery stables. His arm had healed enough that it didn't cause him as much pain as he moved. He'd stopped taking the laudanum at night for the pain because it made him sleep too heavily and took away his appetite in the morning. Instead, he was making a small cup of tea in the evening when Brown Bear stopped into the Sheriff's Office and brought him willow bark to use for the pain instead. It didn't taste all that great, but it was a good alternative to the medicine. And since he now had a handle on the pain, he was eager to gain back his ability to ride a horse so he could do patrols around town instead of relying on Tanner for everything.

Jacob had just managed to pull himself up into the saddle with much strain when Tanner came hurrying into the corral. At first, he thought something might have happened, but Tanner pulled a letter out of his back pocket and flashed it at Jacob as a big grin came onto his face.

"Guess what just rolled in on the stagecoach," Tanner said as he approached him. Jacob leaned over a bit, grabbed the letter out of Tanner's extended arm and looked to see that the letter came from Boston. He could only assume it was Rosa and he was relieved to think she'd written him after he'd constructed his last letter so poorly.

"She must see something in you," Tanner said with a wink, his hands on his hips. Jacob gave him a smirk before he tucked the letter in his back pocket, which was a difficult task when he had to lean forward on the saddle without bracing himself on the saddle horn because his only good arm was being used to tuck in the letter. But since he'd been riding horses all his life, he was able to keep his balance.

"Well, there is only one way to find out," Jacob said as he steered his horse towards the outer portion of the corral with the intent of doing some different maneuvers before heading over to the inn for supper.

"You sure you should be riding?" Tanner called after him as he stood in the center of the ring. "Dr. Harvey made it my responsibility to make sure you didn't get yourself into any more trouble."

"Then you shouldn't be distracting me," Jacob shot back, the words out of his mouth before he could really think about what he was saying. He sighed then as he placed his attention on putting his horse through the paces. First, they cantered and trotted around the ring, then Jacob started to do loops and barrel turns to make sure his horse was still getting all the exercise he needed to stay fit and ready for action. But even though Jacob was able to move with his horse, he found it harder to do sharp turns with only one hand. Eventually, Jacob led his horse into the livery stable and dismounted slowly, handing the reins over to a stable boy before meeting back up with Tanner.

"That was harder than it should be," Jacob admitted as he stood there breathing hard. Riding one handed had taken it out of him more than he'd expected. He almost considered skipping dinner and going straight to bed, but he knew that skipping out on a meal wouldn't help him in the long run. And since Jacob had been forced to sleep on his back instead of his right side like he preferred, sleep wasn't exactly easy to come by anymore.

"Well, why don't I go grab us something to eat from the inn and you can read that letter and tell me about it," Tanner offered.

"My goodness, you are as nosey as Mayor Franklin," Jacob quipped with a chuckle. Tanner blew out a deep breath as he rolled his eyes in response.

"I'm simply trying to keep a good eye on you like Dr. Harvey expects of me," Tanner retorted. "I'm providing you with a meal and in return I can be someone you can talk to if need be."

"And that's why I keep you around, Tanner. You're a good man," Jacob said as he turned to leave the corral and make his way back to the Sheriff's Office. "I'll see you in a bit. Make sure to bring pie with you."

"You're going to lose your good looks if all you eat is pie," Tanner called back to him. Jacob just shrugged his shoulders and continued on his way, eager to read Rosa's letter. As Jacob made it back to the office, saying hello to all that he passed, he was starting to feel the weight of having ridden too hard too soon. He plopped down in his chair at his desk and took a few minutes to just breathe before he took out Rosa's letter and began to read it.

DEAR JACOB BENNING,

I was pleased to receive your letter. I will admit that at first I was appalled by your handwriting, but once I was able to understand why you were using your left hand, I couldn't help but chuckle. The image of a strong sheriff who doesn't let anything get in his way was replaced by an image of a normal human being who could fall ill from time to time. I hope that you are able to rest often and that your right arm is speedily healing. It must be difficult not to use your predominant hand, making simple tasks more difficult. I will say that I did try to write a few words with my left hand and saw how terribly frustrating it is. So, I am glad that you took the time to reply to my letter instead of waiting to use your right hand again.

The weather in Boston is quite lovely this time of year. The days are warm and I often try to spend as much time outside as possible. Growing up in the orphanage, the gardens and outside space were not well kept so it wasn't always fun to be outside. But the gardens of the Trevino family are well kept and quite beautiful. I like to think I could keep a garden this beautiful one day and teach my children all about plants and flowers. I understand that having a decent garden is ideal for surviving in the West and I can say honestly that it is something I would look forward to if I were to come out West.

Though I was an orphan without any knowledge of who my parents were, I like to think I've created a decent life for myself here in Boston. I possess many domestic skills that I don't mind at all. I've never dreamed of having my own servants, but perhaps just a family to tend to and a husband instead of a lady of society. I know that by moving to Bear Creek I will miss some things about Boston, but I don't think it would compare to fulfilling my desire to marry for love and have a large family one day.

Well, that's enough about me. I hope that you'll respond with the happen-

ings of Bear Creek as of late. I promise not to laugh the entire time I am
trying to read your next letter.

    Rosa Casey

JACOB CHUCKLED as he folded up the letter and set it on his desk. He was pleased to learn that at least Rosa had a good sense of humor. He couldn't imagine what it would be like to grow up without parents. He had been raised by two wonderful parents who had him later in life. Though they were both passed away now, he still had many fond memories of growing up on a farm. Sometimes he dearly missed his parents, and other times he had to remind himself that he had good support from the people of Bear Creek as well.

Tanner came into the Sheriff's Office just as he was about to start writing his response letter. He grumbled underneath his breath as he put the paper and ink pot away. The moment he smelled the food that Tanner had brought with him, he figured he'd eat first and write later once he'd thought more about what he actually wanted to write.

"Mrs. Tibet has really cooked up a treat tonight," Tanner said as he set a basket on his desk and started to pull out various items. "I told her how much you enjoy her pies, so she sent over a shepherd's pie and a custard pie just for you." Jacob raised his eyebrows, thinking that Mrs. Tibet was being very generous today.

"I don't know where the woman finds all the energy to bake and cook for so many," Jacob said as he put away his letter and focused on eating the food. The moment Tanner gave him a fork, he started to dig in. Tanner just chuckled as he took his dinner over to his own desk.

"Funny you should say that," Tanner said as he settled down into his chair. "Mr. Tibet was saying how good business was with all the new miners in town and that Mrs. Tibet was having a hard time manning the kitchen all on her own."

"Really?" Jacob asked, surprised by the news. "I'm glad to hear the inn is successful again, but I never imagined Mrs. Tibet would have trouble feeding so many."

"Well, the couple is getting older, and with their children long gone, it's just the two of them to do all the work," Tanner explained. "Perhaps your mail-order-bride would be interested in a cooking position." Jacob thought about it for a moment, thinking that at least it wouldn't hurt to ask. He ate his dinner, thinking over a few things since he wanted to reply to Rosa as soon as he could.

As Jacob thought about Rosa's two letters, he thought he had a good feeling about her. She was willing to work hard despite how the beginning of her life had started. She seemed to be happy with what she was doing and at least had considered what it would be like to live in the West from a reasonable perspective. It would be good for Jacob to already have some sort of employment for Rosa before she arrived in town, and he'd have to ask around to see if anyone had an extra room for her. The inn would no doubt be booked already by the miners, but perhaps Mathew and Jenny would like the company? But would that really work if Rosa was all the way out of town?

At the end of the meal, Jacob at least knew one thing. He wanted to write back to Rosa, and he wanted her to come to Bear Creek. He figured he could iron out the details when she arrived. Just the thought of inviting Rosa to Bear Creek with the intention of marrying filled him with excitement. He dearly hoped that he had finally found the one whom he could fall in love with and start a family with.

CHAPTER 5

*R*osa was in the kitchen preparing Katelyn one of her favorite treats when one of the footmen popped into the kitchen to deliver her a letter before going on his way. She didn't need to read the address on the letter to see who had written it. She only had ever received letters from one person and smiled as she quickly tucked it into her apron pocket so she wouldn't get flour on it. Rosa had always enjoyed cooking and when she'd first been brought into the household, she'd learned many things to include cooking Katelyn's favorite meals. Therefore, she was currently rolling out biscuit dough to make Katelyn her favorite shortbread with jam.

"If I have to hear another complaint come out of that woman's mouth, I'm going to quit," Mrs. Weatherlore said as she came bustling into the kitchen. She was the housekeeper over the entire estate and often had to deal with Mrs. Trevino on a personal basis all day long. Rosa had no desire to ever be a housekeeper for the Trevino family and had declined any promotions even though she had acquired many different skills. She not only prepared tea the best out of any of the maids, but she also cooked wonderfully. When Cook ever became ill or too sick to cook, Rosa would always substitute for her till she recovered in addition to her other duties.

"What has happened now?" Cook asked. She was working beside Rosa making rolls for the evening meal while a joint roasted in the oven.

"Mrs. Trevino requested new place settings for tonight's dinner party at the manor," Mrs. Weatherlore said as she took a few deep breaths to settle her racing heart. She knew she shouldn't let her temper get the best of her, but today was proving to be difficult for the housekeeper.

"I placed the order and set them myself this afternoon. But the woman said that they are the wrong ones, that I made a mistake and now must use the old ones," Mrs. Weatherlore exclaimed. "And I don't have time to change them back."

"What other duties do you have?" Rosa asked, hoping she could be of some help to the older woman. She didn't like how Mrs. Trevino often treated the servants and would go out of her way to help the other women in service.

"I must go and fetch Mrs. Trevino's new gown from the seamstress and check with Mr. Long if there are any radishes in the garden because the woman insists that the color red would heighten the salad for this evening. And with it only being spring, I doubt there are any radishes and therefore I must go to the market to look for some," Mrs. Weatherlore said in a very fast pace to the point where she needed to take a deep breath to steady herself once more.

"I'll take care of those errands, you go change the place settings. Cook, I'll leave you to look after the shortbreads in the oven," Rosa said as she began to wipe her hands clean.

"My goodness, you are a Godsend, Miss Casey," Mrs. Weatherlore said as she drank down a cup of water before hurrying back out of the kitchen.

"You certainly set yourself up this afternoon," Cook commented as she shaped her bread rolls.

"I won't be needed till this evening to dress Miss Trevino. If I spend less than an hour out of the house, all should be well," Rosa replied. She took a few coins from the servant's box for running errands and hurried to the back door where she pulled on her cloak before heading outside. Since it was such short notice, Rosa didn't bother requesting that one of the footmen take her into the city on one of the pull carts. Instead, she hailed a petty cab and was on her way in a matter of minutes.

While she waited to be taken to the seamstress, Rosa pulled the letter from Jacob from her pocket. She chuckled as she noticed that the letter had been addressed to her in nice, clear handwriting. But when she pulled the letter open, she saw the same awful handwriting from before. It took her some time, but she had a few minutes to spare as the petty cab waded through traffic to deliver her to where she needed to go. Rosa read each word carefully, her heart quickening as she continued reading more.

DEAR ROSA,

There have been a few showers this spring in Bear Creek, but nothing disastrous. I always love the smell of the town after the rain. Everything always smells so clean and new after a good rainstorm. With so many miners coming to town, the inn here has become quite busy. My deputy has just explained that Mrs. Tibet, who manages the inn with her husband, has become quite busy since she also cooks for the guests and whomever wants to come in for a meal. The inn would be our version of a restaurant since most families cook their own meals. But every once in a while it's nice to eat somewhere else. And since my right arm has been broken, I've probably frequented the inn more often than I should.

What I am trying to say is that Mrs. Tibet could use help at the inn with cooking the meals and serving the guests. If you are ready, I'd like you to come out to Bear Creek at your earliest convenience to not only offer your services to Mrs. Tibet, but also with the intention of marrying me. I assure you that I won't pressure you to marry me unless we really hit it off. If things don't work out for us, there are plenty of other single men in Bear Creek that you could probably have your pick.

I hope you'll reply with your agreement to come to Bear Creek, and we shall see how things go from there. I'm not too fond of cats, but I'm willing to give our relationship a try.

Jacob Benning

ROSA WAS a little shocked by the forwardness of the letter. She had assumed that they would exchange letters for at least a year before he would request that she come out West. But it was good to know that she might have employment before she even arrived. She couldn't help but chuckle at Jacob's admittance that he wasn't keen on cats. Rosa simply appreciated that the Sheriff was being honest with her, and therefore she couldn't fault him for that. She found it difficult, though, to think of leaving Katelyn. Despite her generous offer of a ticket to Montana, Rosa knew that Katelyn relied on her in so many ways.

Rosa banished any thought of Montana as the petty cab stopped in front of the seamstress' shop. She asked the driver to wait for her a moment as she stepped down and hurried inside to collect Mrs. Trevino's gown. Once that task was complete, she asked the driver to take her to the market so she could hopefully find some radishes. Rosa reflected on how easy it was to live in Boston because everything she needed was a short trip across town. She had good employment already and actually enjoyed what she did.

By some miracle, there was a small bundle of radishes in the marketplace. Rosa quickly paid for them before heading back to the petty cab. Once the driver returned her home, she paid him generously before taking her two bundles in through the servant's door. She stopped in the kitchen to deposit the radishes, much to Cook's joy. The other woman assured her that the shortbread had been baked, so Rosa then went further into the house to give Mrs. Weatherlore the gown. She found the housekeeper in the dining room, fussing over the table placements.

"Here you are, Mrs. Weatherlore," Rosa said as she came into the room. The woman turned at the sound of her voice and smiled brightly as she took the gown.

"Oh, Miss Casey. You have no idea how much this means to me," Mrs. Weatherlore said as she quickly patted her shoulder and headed out of the room. "The woman better be pleased now." Rosa couldn't help but laugh as she watched the woman go. She then returned to the kitchen to collect a small plate of shortbread before taking it up to Katelyn's room.

When Rosa knocked on the bedroom door, Katelyn was quick to bid her enter. She was sitting in front of her looking glass, turning her head left to right as she viewed her own reflection. Rosa smiled at her as she came into the room, closed the door behind her and then set the plate of biscuits on the serving table in the room.

"Rosa, do you think I look any different today?" Katelyn asked as she turned to her lady-in-waiting. Rosa came over to her then and looked down at her friend, trying to see what Katelyn was referring to.

"No, I don't think so," Rosa admitted before heading over to her wardrobe and preparing her outfit for the evening.

"I am a changed girl," Katelyn said happily. "I went and told that Fredrick what I think of him."

Rosa was too stunned to speak for a moment. Then, "You must have given him a shock," she said, smiling.

"Not only him. His fiancée was with him."

"Oh, Katelyn! What happened?"

"I left her screaming at him and at all their friends." Katelyn bit the side of her thumb, a habit she had whenever she had behaved badly.

Before Rosa could say anything the door opened and Mrs. Trevino entered. Her dark eyes were flashing. Katelyn had once told Rosa that her mother was half Italian and half Irish. "The mixture makes her lose control sometimes. Then she has to go and lie down but not before she has taken my father and me apart.'

"Katelyn, I have just had the most extraordinary visit from Mrs. Buckmaster. She says you insulted her daughter and told her a catalogue of lies about her fiancé; that young Fredrick, I told you not to encourage. Is this true?"

Rosa was proud of the way Katelyn drew herself up and looked her mother in the eye. "I told Maisie the truth, that Fredrick is a liar and a breaker of hearts and if she had any sense she would hand him back his ring." She paused for a moment then continued in a lower voice, "I didn't know she was going to be there, or anyone else; I just wanted to tell Fredrick what a cad he is." She stumbled, then flung her arms in the air and added with a cry, "I loved him!"

Rosa was taken aback. She had thought Katelyn's feelings for Fredrick had been no more than a young girl's romantic fling; passionate but fleeting.

Mrs. Trevino looked coldly at her daughter. "We have this dinner tonight, I have no time to deal with you now. You will not go out tonight and tomorrow I shall tell you exactly what must happen." She then turned to Rosa. "I blame you for this. If you had been attending to your duties properly, this disgraceful episode would never have happened and Katelyn would not now be the talk of Boston."

"I didn't know all those other people were going to be there!" Katelyn said, tears beginning to pour down her face. "It was just supposed to be Fredrick. Only I couldn't stop myself."

Rosa put her arms around the weeping girl.

"I have thought for some time that you were a bad influence on Katelyn," Mrs. Trevino said coldly to Rosa. "I should never have taken you out of that orphanage. Your employment in this house is at an end. You will leave tomorrow."

"Mother!" Katelyn wailed. "You can't mean that! Rosa had nothing to do with this afternoon. She can't leave. She's my best friend."

Mrs. Trevino rose, her taffeta skirts whispering around her as she turned to leave the room. "Tomorrow!' she said in an awful voice and left.

Katelyn collapsed in Rosa's arms. 'She can't mean it. You can't leave me. How will I know what to wear!"

Rosa had to smile. Katelyn was genuinely upset but her first thought was for her appearance. Her own thoughts were in a turmoil. Had she really just lost her job? The whole household knew how vindictive Mrs. Trevino could be but Katelyn and Rosa were so close. Then she wondered, could the woman be jealous of how close her daughter was to the lady's maid whose origins were an orphanage?

"Papa will say you must stay," Katelyn collected herself. "He knows how important you are in my life. Now, brush my hair and tell me what I should wear tomorrow. I must look my very best to show everyone I am who I am."

Rosa smiled and picked up the hair brush. That was Katelyn, nothing was going to keep her down.

LATER THAT EVENING, after Rosa had arranged for supper to be brought to the two of them in Katelyn's room, she told her about Jacob's letter and his invitation.

Katelyn clapped her hands. "That's marvelous! You can write back immediately and say you are coming. It doesn't matter if Papa doesn't tell Mother you have to stay, I shall tell them you are off to a new life." She leaned forward and took Rosa's hand in hers. "I said I would pay for your fare out there, and back again if things don't work out. I've got all that money Grandmama left me. It was to be mine after my seventeenth birthday. Well, that was a while ago and I still haven't spent any of it. Paying for you to go to Montana will be no more than small change." She released Rosa's hand and flung her arms around her. "Oh, I will miss you so much but it will be wonderful to think of you living in Montana. You will send me long letters and let me know how everything is there. Where is Montana? Tomorrow we must find a map and see how far away it is."

Rosa felt the warmth of Katelyn's embrace and some of the shock of Mrs. Trevino's words left her.

"This is fantastic news," Katelyn said as Rosa settled her down for the night after they had spent the rest of the evening trying to imagine what life in Bear Creek might be like. "Now you can travel to the West and marry the man of your dreams." Her enthusiasm was so overwhelming that all Rosa could do was chuckle in response.

"I wish I had your excitement," Rosa said starting to feel a little nervous "But I am glad that Jacob feels confident to invite me to come to Bear Creek and has already passed along possible employment." Rosa cleared away Katelyn's discarded clothes and placed their supper dishes outside the door. then said, "And he isn't very fond of cats."

"I understand that you have some reservations but I haven't heard you state anything that should keep you from the opportunity to love a man who could one day be your husband."

Rosa thought that Katelyn was giving her some pretty sound advice. It seemed her life in Boston could be at an end and, though she was nervous about leaving Boston and traveling for two weeks to Montana while trying to transport her cat, the possibilities of what could be waiting for her in Bear Creek, to include everything she had always dreamed about, was simply too good to pass up. After all, Katelyn had already promised her that if things did not work out that she could always come back to Boston.

"What I am going to do," Katelyn spoke up then as Rosa became lost in thought and the task at hand, "is talk to my father tomorrow and tell him that you have gained an employment position in Montana that you simply cannot refuse. Then, tomorrow we shall go shopping for your trip so that you are well prepared. And before you go, I shall have Papa write you a wonderful recommendation letter."

"You really think Mr. Trevino will do that for me?" Rosa asked, surprised by the idea. "After what Mrs. Trevino said?"

"Rosa, I can fend for myself and there are plenty of other maids who can assist me," Katelyn urged. "Even if they don't have your gift for fashion. Don't give up on your dream just because my mother has taken it into her head you must leave."

Rosa lay in bed that night not knowing exactly what to think. She was excited about the idea of moving to Bear Creek and meeting Jacob in person, but Boston was the only place she'd ever known and she wasn't sure if she'd enjoy living in a remote town. She didn't doubt her skills to survive and tend to a house, but would she enjoy living outside a big city? Then she knew, that even though she was comfortable living in Boston, she wouldn't be able to fulfill her dream of having a large family here.

Finally Rosa got out of bed, lit the lamp and wrote her letter to Jacob telling him she was arranging to come to Bear Creek. She sealed the envelope and sat for a moment thinking of all the newspaper stories that said living in the West was a difficult feat, that it would take time to travel to Bear Creek, that life there was much harder, and that survival depended on how hard you worked. Rosa was used to working hard to please the family she worked for, but would she be able to do the same thing for her husband and children without all the resources she was used to?

Rosa eventually had to tell her mind to stop worrying so much and just have a little faith in Jacob. After all, he'd been born and raised in the West and had grown up to live a good life and now had a good position within the community. Furthermore, Bear Creek sounded like the type of community where everyone worked together so that no one ever went without. Rosa had to put her trust in the fact that her destiny was leading her to Bear Creek and she should just respect the fact that she'd been given such a great opportunity.

She picked up Sheba, her tabby-cat, and held her to her chest, despite the cat's protests of being woken up from a perfectly good nap.

"We're moving to Montana," Rosa said in a sing-song voice to the cat as she sat down on her bed and petted her feline companion. "And I'm sure you'll have all the space in the world to roam free." Sheba meowed loudly, signaling that she was ready to be put down. Rosa set her down and saw her leap out the open window. Rosa thought how wonderful it must be to be a cat and not have to worry about anything but a good meal.

THE NEXT WEEK seemed to fly by for Rosa as she and Katelyn worked together to prepare her for her trip. Mrs. Trevino had not changed her mind about firing Rosa but Mr. Trevino had not only written Rosa a letter of recommendation but had paid her a bonus for her dedicated service for over a decade to the Trevino family. Rosa was surprised by the money, especially after Mrs. Trevino's attitude. She tried to ignore the woman's sour mood; it wasn't difficult because Katelyn had kept her promise and taken Rosa to get all the things she would need for living in the West without expecting Rosa to pay for a thing.

"You'll need day gowns, working gowns, riding gowns, and traveling gowns," Katelyn declared during their day of shopping. "You'll probably need at least three trunks and a special carrier for Sheba."

"Are you certain this will all be necessary?" Rosa asked as Katelyn took her to the seamstress. Rosa had never purchased a new gown before or ever been fitted for one. It was a new experience all together that Rosa thought was very enjoyable.

"I am absolutely certain," Katelyn urged as she had all manner of gowns made up for Rosa and insisted that the order be finished as soon as possible. The gowns alone cost a fortune, but at every purchase Katelyn only continued to reassure Rosa that her father would think the gowns were for her and wouldn't bat an eye at the cost.

With everything packed away in three trunks and Sheba tucked away inside a carrier that was designed for birds, causing the tabby-cat to become quite frustrated, Rosa finally stood on the train station platform next to Katelyn thinking that all of this had happened rather suddenly, and as she held Katelyn's hands in hers, she tried very hard not to cry.

"As soon as you can, please write me," Katelyn said as she tried to keep her composure. Rosa had always been her lady's maid, but it wasn't until she had to say goodbye did she realize just how close of a friend she'd become to her over the years. And no matter how saddened Katelyn would be to see her go, she was truly happy for Rosa and her chance to escape the overbearing city of Boston.

"I shall write you at every availability. I shall let you know that I am well and that I've fallen madly in love with Jacob and we are going to have ten babies," Rosa said with a chuckle. She made herself smile even though all she wanted to do was hold her friend tight. It would be no use for them if she began to cry now. After all, she had a train to catch.

Katelyn had paid for Rosa's train ticket and all her travel expenses, including a private compartment on the train. Two attendants came and took her trunks on board and then waited to show Rosa to her compartment. Knowing the time had come, she finally pulled Katelyn into a tight embrace.

"Remember what I told you, Katelyn. Make a man work for your heart and guard it till he does so," Rosa said. She then released her oldest friend and looked into her eyes. "And you must promise to write me as well."

"I promise," Katelyn said as a tear slipped from her eye. She moved quickly to wipe it away, never wanting to appear emotional in public. "Now be gone with you. I don't wish to see you again unless you've come to show me your handsome husband."

"As you wish, my dear," Rosa said as she picked up Sheba's carrier, waved goodbye one last time, and then turned and followed the attendants onto the train. Rosa was instantly aware of how small and narrow the train was. With everyone boarding the train at once, she had to walk sideways at times to get around passengers until she was shown her own compartment. She was overly thankful in that moment to have her own space on the train. She couldn't imagine traveling for two weeks in the open compartments that served all the other travelers.

As soon as all her trunks were situated and she was bid farewell by the attendants, the compartment doors were closed and Rosa was given time to herself. She looked out the window at the train platform to see if she could see Katelyn. But it appeared as if the young woman had left, perhaps not being able to bear to watch the train take off. Rosa didn't blame her, feeling her own heart heavy with the thought of never seeing her best friend again.

When the train whistle blew three times, the train lurched forward, causing Rosa to clutch on the side of the plush bench seat. Sheba meowed loudly, not liking the feeling of the train, either. It took a few minutes for the train to gain speed and steadily rumble down the tracks, the sensation very jarring to Rosa. She did her best to just focus on her breathing as she watched the train station start to pass by the window. It seemed like seconds before the station was completely gone, followed by the city as a forest came up to greet the train. Rosa was so transfixed by the changing scenery that she didn't hear someone knock on the compartment door.

"Come in!" Rosa called when the knock came a second time. An attendant opened the door then and dipped his head.

"Excuse me, miss. I'm checking everyone's tickets," the attendant explained. Rosa fished out her train ticket from her small purse that was fastened to her wrist. She handed it over to the attendant who punched a hole in it with a small clicker before handing it back to Rosa. "Pardon for the interruption. Meals are served in the dining car at the back of the train. First stop will be in about an hour." Then the attendant stepped out of the compartment before shutting the door once more.

Rosa sighed heavily as she reached down towards the cat carrier and pulled up the latch, allowing Sheba to scamper out. She ran around the small compartment for a moment before settling down on the seat beside Rosa. Watching Sheba took her mind off the movement of the train, which she was finding difficult in becoming used to. Instead, she simply kept an eye on her cat and took in the details of the compartment.

There was a single train window with latches that would allow her to open it if need be. Rosa didn't think that would be necessary and perhaps a bit dangerous if she were to do so. But if it became so hot at night that she couldn't sleep well, she'd be willing to give it a go. Speaking of sleeping, Rosa tried to imagine how she would achieve that while the train was traveling down the tracks. Perhaps they stopped at night to allow passengers an opportunity for decent sleep? But Rosa figured that then it would take forever to reach Montana. Looking around, Rosa saw how the bottoms of the two benches lifted up and connected to form a makeshift bed, and the storage above the other bench included linens, pillows, and blankets.

Overall, Rosa figured that she was quite lucky to have an entire compartment to herself. She could give Sheba some exercise and she'd packed plenty of old newspapers to give Sheba a place to do her business on. Whatever food she purchased on the train or at stops she'd also use to feed the cat. And with any luck, they'd both arrive safe and sound in Montana and be able to start a new life together. But as Sheba started to scratch at the door, wanting out, Rosa knew that she'd have her hands full with the tabby-cat. At least without any position to keep her busy, she could give all her attention to her cat and try to make them both comfortable.

After a while, Rosa decided it couldn't hurt to venture out of the compartment for a little while. She brought only one novel to occupy her time with, and since she didn't think she could read on the train till she got used to its rocking, she decided she'd try venturing out and walking up and down the train to gain her bearings. Once Rosa was able to coax Sheba back into the carrier, Rosa stood on wobbly legs and moved towards the door, slowly opening it and taking a step out into the narrow corridor.

When she closed the door behind her, Rosa looked up and down the train. She seemed to be in a train car that only contained compartments. She walked back the way she had first come onto the train, and after passing through various cars, she came into a more general portion where many people occupied seats that took up most of the car. Rosa didn't want to appear nosey or to stare at any particular person, so she simply placed a pleasant expression on her face and walked up the aisle, trying to walk without tripping over herself. It was a hard task to accomplish since the train was constantly rocking back and forth.

Eventually, Rosa found the dining cart. It was filled with small tables and chairs that appeared to have been nailed down to the floor to prevent them from moving. A small kitchen occupied one part of the car with a stove whose chimney poked through the top of the roof. Rosa could see the sky peeking in through the hole and she dearly hoped that it didn't rain during their travels or perhaps there wouldn't be any cooked food on the train.

"Can I help you, miss?" one of the attendants asked her, a young man with sandy brown hair. He was standing behind the counter, seeming to be doing some prep work for the next meal.

"No, I'm just getting familiar with the train is all," Rosa explained as she looked around. It was charmingly designed, and if it hadn't been for the movement of the train, she would have thought it was very inviting.

"First time ever traveling by train?" the attendant asked, giving her a kind smile. His blue eyes sparkled, and she could tell that this young man could be trouble for any unaccompanied young lady. But even though Rosa was traveling alone, her heart was only set on one man, and that was Jacob Benning.

"Yes, this is my first time traveling by train. By first observation, I find it rather exhausting," Rosa said as she gripped onto one of the chairs to balance herself when the train jarred around a bend. The attendant laughed as he continued prepping his food as though he'd felt nothing.

"Depending how long you have to go, you'll get used to the movement of the train," the attendant said as he worked. "My name's Philip, by the way."

"Charmed," was all Rosa was willing to say as she dipped her head and turned around, intent on returning to her own compartment. She saw no need to share names with the man and figured she was giving him a good enough sign that she wasn't in the mood for making his acquaintance. If Katelyn had taught her anything over the years, it was how to act like a lady and make sure others understood that you are a lady through and through. Rosa was insistent on acting as a lady at every opportunity to make people question her position in society. If they never knew who she really was, she was free to pretend to be whomever she felt like.

Rosa returned to her compartment to the sound of Sheba meowing for her. She didn't want to disturb any of the other passengers in the nearby compartments, so she let her out of her carrier once more and gave her a small bite of the biscuits Cook had made for her journey. Rosa had to search through her trunks to find that small box of goodies, and as she sat and ate a few, she realized that she'd worked with many great people within the Trevino household. She could only hope that they would all find happiness in their lives, and she secretly hoped that she soon would, too.

CHAPTER 6

*I*n the middle of the night, Rosa woke for what seemed like the hundredth time. Anytime the train would jar one way or another, she was startled awake. She imagined that even sleeping on a ship wouldn't have been this complicated. She tried changing position on the makeshift bed, but still couldn't get comfortable enough to sleep. And since Sheba constantly cried now every time she was placed in her carrier, she'd let the cat out before going to bed, thinking the feline would snuggle with her. But the cat had only continued to look for a way out.

"Sheba, where are you girl?" Rosa whispered, wanting to feel comforted by her companion. But as she sat up in bed and felt around for her, she was starting to panic when she couldn't feel the animal anywhere near her. Thinking that Sheba must have been hiding underneath the bed, Rosa laid back down and willed herself to fall back to sleep. She pulled the covers up over her head and prayed that sleep would come easier to her this time.

Come morning, Rosa felt more exhausted than when she'd gone to bed the previous night. She sat up, her body stiff from tensing at every little bump in the train. She rubbed the sleep out of her eyes before stretching her arms over her head. She grumbled when she heard the whistle of the train sound three times, signaling that the train was coming into a station. And since Rosa was not up and ready, she wouldn't be able to depart the train for a short reprieve from her small compartment. She'd been able to the day before and found how delightful it was to take a short walk into a new place. The train stopped for a total of thirty minutes at each station, giving her enough time to take a quick peek, make any food purchases she wanted, and get back on the train before it departed. But since she had slept in, she knew she wouldn't be able to have enough time at this stop.

Taking her time, Rosa rose from the bed and began to pull off the linens to store overhead so she could fold the bed back up. After she'd done so, she looked around for Sheba, wondering where she could be. She peered into the carrier and saw she wasn't there and started to wonder if Sheba could have escaped the compartment..

Rosa began to panic as she quickly dressed and combed her hair before braiding it in a hurry. She knew she didn't look the best she could, which Katelyn would have determined was unsuitable for her, but Rosa didn't really care about appearances at the moment. She was desperate to find her cat and ensure the tabby was alright.

She stepped into the corridor and closed the door behind her before looking both ways up and down, hoping to see the cat right outside her door. She then began steadily looking for Sheba everywhere, even going to the different cars as though the cat could open doors or pass between the cars. Rosa couldn't comprehend how Sheba had gotten out of her compartment, and with most passengers off the train while it was still in the station, she took the opportunity to bend down and look underneath seats or up above in storage areas.

"Where have you gone?" Rosa mumbled to herself once she reached the end of the train. She'd reached the dining cart, and after looking around quickly, she determined that Sheba was nowhere to be found. Feeling defeated and thoroughly dejected, she settled down into a chair at an empty table and simply sat and stared out the window. Was losing her dearly loved cat an omen for her journey? Were all her hopes for this venture going to fall apart?

"What can I get you today, miss?" asked the attendant she'd met the day before. She thought she remembered his name as being Philip, but she really didn't care at that moment.

"I'd like a cup of tea and some toast, please," Rosa said, not even bothering to look up at the man.

"I'm sorry, miss, but all we have is coffee at the moment. The further the train gets from the East, the less tea is readily available," the attendant explained. Rosa felt tears pricking the edges of her eyes as she wondered how much worse this day could get.

"I'll take a cup of coffee with plenty of milk and sugar then. And jam on the toast, please," Rosa responded.

"Certainly. I'll have that whipped up for you in a moment," Phillip replied before darting behind the counter and preparing the order.

Rosa was starting to wonder if traveling out West was really the best idea. Now she was without her companion and more exhausted than she'd ever been in her life. Once she'd stayed up all night long when Katelyn had caught a cold. She had kept a cool cloth on her head all night to break the fever and drawn a bath for her in the morning so that the steam could help with her stuffy nose. But now she felt worse than she ever had in her entire life.

After enjoying the decent cup of coffee and toast, Rosa paid for the meal and then headed back to her compartment. She searched every inch of the space once more before settling down on the bench and looking outside the window. Sound reverberated through the train once more as passengers filed on in a hurry, the sound of chatter, laughter, and shouting filling her ears before the train started to move forward. Rosa realized how many days of traveling were ahead of her and wasn't sure if she would be able to arrive in Bear Creek with the same optimistic point of view as she had when she first boarded the train yesterday.

JACOB PACED BACK and forth on the front porch of Fry's mercantile store, waiting for the afternoon stagecoach to come in. He'd received a telegram from Rosa stating that she'd be arriving in town this day.

Now, Jacob was trying to wait patiently for her but couldn't sit still long enough to do so. His right arm had started to become rather itchy underneath the plaster and Dr. Harvey assured him that it was all part of the healing process. Jacob wanted to rip the cast off and scratch his skin till it was raw but doing so would probably set back his healing another month. So, Jacob had to do his best to keep his mind off the state of his arm so that he could get things done each day.

A plume of dust rose up in the distance as Jacob looked down the road that led out of town heading East. At first, he thought it was just a dust twister. But as it continued to build, he realized that the stage-coach was finally coming into town. Jacob raised his left hand up to his brow, shielding the sun from his eyes so he could get a good look at it. He was eager to meet Rosa and had dressed in his official uniform as a sheriff. He didn't wear the black jacket and trousers often, but he really wanted to give Rosa a good impression right off the bat.

The moment the stagecoach came rumbling into town and the driver pulled the horses to a rapid stop, the man was down in a flash to start pulling goods and cargo from the stagecoach as Jacob stepped forward and pulled open the door. He poked his head in and saw a young lady with blonde hair and deep brown eyes trying to smooth down the skirt of her dress. She looked rather lovely in a pale blue gown and he could tell right away she wasn't from a place anywhere like Bear Creek.

"I assume you are Miss Rosa Casey," Jacob said with a grin. Rosa looked at the person that had addressed her, surprised to see a very handsome gentleman instead of the stagecoach driver she'd met on departing from the train early that morning. This gentleman had sandy-blond hair, dazzling blue eyes, and a grin that showed that he had a pretty good set of teeth. And when she saw that his right arm was casted and resting in a sling, she was confident of who this man was.

"Sheriff Jacob Benning, I would presume," Rosa said with a kind smile. She was thoroughly exhausted from all her troubles and still heartbroken over losing Sheba. But she was pleased to see that at least Jacob was both handsome and punctual.

"May I help you down from the stagecoach?" Jacob offered as he extended his left hand towards her. Rosa nodded and accepted his help as she stepped down from the vehicle, pleased to leave the other passengers she'd been squeezed up with, especially a loudly dressed woman who seemed to be no better than she ought and had a dreadful cough. Pleased also to know that she wouldn't have to ride in another stagecoach or train for as long as she lived. Or at least as long as things worked out between her and Jacob.

"Well then, how was your trip?" Jacob asked once they were both standing on the porch of the mercantile. He saw Rosa looking all around, taking in her new surroundings. The other woman in the coach had also gotten out and was trying to deal with a hacking cough. Jacob looked at her and knew she was trouble. Even as he thought of approaching her and finding out what her business was, he saw Mr. Cricket, who ran the seedy boarding house patronized by the miners who hadn't managed to secure accommodation in the Inn. The man, a wretched specimen, weedy, his clothes something out of the charity basket, came up to the woman.

She pulled her arm from his grasp. "You leave me alone, understand?"

"Of course, dear."

"Marge come?"

"Arrived day before yesterday. Having a great time."

"We should have come together. We're mates, see? Only I had a job to do."

"And now you'll be working together," Cricket said in the smarmy voice that Jacob could never bear to listen to. He knew what they were talking about. The man had arranged 'entertainment' for the miners in his boarding house. Jacob had seen the other woman, Marge, arrive and had wanted to send her right back where she'd come from. Only even the Sheriff couldn't do that without some reason. As it was, Cricket would claim the two women were helping with the housework. Housework his eye!

Jacob forgot about Cricket and his doxies and turned his attention back to Rosa. "I am surely glad to meet with you at last," he said, feasting his eyes on her lovely face. "I hope the journey here hasn't been too difficult."

Rosa gave a sigh of relief. Jacob really seemed overjoyed to see her. Rosa didn't want to appear rude so she turned her attention back to the person she was potentially supposed to be marrying.

"I won't try to hide the truth that traveling by train and stagecoach is absolutely horrendous," Rosa said with a chuckle. Jacob joined her as he nodded, knowing what it was like. He'd had to travel by train a few times to meet with other sheriffs and the marshal of the territory. He didn't like that mode of transportation either.

"And the worst part is that I lost track of Sheba, my dear cat, during the first night on the train," Rosa explained with a deep sigh. "I have no idea how she got out of the compartment or what happened to her." A part of Jacob was sorry for Rosa but at the same time he was kind of glad that he wouldn't have to deal with the cat.

"I'm sorry to hear all of this, Rosa," Jacob said with a sympathetic smile. "I hope you come to love Bear Creek as much as I do and you'll find that coming all the way out here was worth it." As Rosa looked up at Jacob and saw the kindness in his face, she was already feeling reassured that this had been the right decision. There was something about Jacob that soothed her and she wondered if this was one of his many talents as a good sheriff.

"Well, I took the liberty of securing a room at the inn for you, Miss Casey. Once I told the Tibets that you'd be interested in helping Mrs. Tibet in the kitchen, they made sure that you'd have a place to stay when you came to town," Jacob said. "Miners have a way of finding a place to stay, even if it's up in the mountain. We didn't think you'd like that."

"I hope I didn't put anyone out," Rosa said. "I'd hate to be the cause of that."

"Don't you worry, Miss Casey. Mr. and Mrs. Tibet wouldn't have done anything like that," Jacob assured. He thought it was kind of Rosa to be considerate of a complete stranger even though she was in need of a place to stay. It showed Jacob that Rosa was truly a kind person and wasn't willing to take advantage of anyone.

"Well, if you say so," Rosa replied as she noticed that her three cases had just been unloaded from the stagecoach. She pointed to them as she said, "Those are my trunks. I don't know how far the inn is from here, but I'd be willing to pay someone to take them over for me." Jacob raised a finger up to Rosa before he took two steps towards the mercantile then poking his head in and yelling for his deputy. Tanner came scurrying out in a hurry, quick to dip his head towards Rosa.

"Rosa, I'd like you to meet my deputy, Tanner Williams," Jacob introduced. "He's a capable young man who'd love nothing more than to take your trunks to your room at the inn." Jacob gave Tanner a pointed look as the deputy's expression said he didn't like the idea of being an errand boy. But since Tanner wanted Jacob to have a real chance at marrying, he didn't say anything more than an 'okay' before making quick work of taking the trunks one at a time over to the inn.

"Well, now that that's taken care of, how about I show you around the town before we make it over to the inn?" Jacob asked as he offered his left arm to Rosa. She smiled kindly at him as she accepted his arm and allowed him to lead her down the boardwalk.

"That was kind of Deputy Tanner to be willing to take my things over," Rosa commented as she looked all around her. She saw that the town was rather small compared to the ones the train had passed through. But she was trying to keep an open mind since this was supposed to be her new home.

"You'll find that many people are like that here in Bear Creek. It's not a large place, but it has all the necessities," Jacob said with a grin as he looked down at her. "The store the stagecoach stops at is the mercantile. Mr. and Mrs. Fry have owned the building since this town was first formed. They have lots of goods, you can pick up your mail there or send a telegram, and Mrs. Fry is a pretty good seamstress." Rosa nodded, slowly taking everything in. She felt exhausted and reasoned that she could look at the town more tomorrow after she'd slept in a proper bed. For now, she was just enjoying not being on a train or in a stagecoach.

"Believe it or not, Bear Creek has a bank," Jacob said as he pointed to the building they were currently passing. "Mr. Louis Fritz opened the bank a few years after the mine opened so miners had a place to sell their gold or store it safely. He's the wealthiest man in town, but things have been hard since the mine went dry. It's only been operational again for about five months and it's really brought business back to the town."

"That is good to know," Rosa said as she peered in through the front door window, seeing a small line of men before the counter. "I have traveled with my life savings and will need to make a deposit before too long."

"Well, Mr. Fritz is a trustworthy guy. You can count on him to keep your money safe. He keeps a rifle behind the counter in case anyone gives him trouble," Jacob assured her. Rosa nodded, thinking that it would probably be reasonable to keep a gun close when you worked at a bank in a remote location. You never knew when someone might come in and rob the place.

"Next we have Mitchel Franks here with his barber shop. He provides a place for miners to get washed up when they come down from the mountains all grimy and covered in mountain dust," Jacob explained as he nodded towards the barbershop, unable to point with his right arm. Rosa didn't bother trying to peer in through the windows. She didn't want to catch sight of any men in the process of getting undressed. Though she'd taken care of Katelyn for years, she'd never seen a man unclothed and didn't want to any time soon unless it was on her wedding night. Rosa then remembered that she was walking arm-in-arm with the man she was intended to and blushed at the thought of seeing him unclothed after they were officially married.

"There's several other places I could show you in town, but I'm sure you're exhausted from your travels," Jacob said as he noticed how quiet Rosa had become. She did look pretty weary even though she had a chipper attitude since getting off the stagecoach. Moving to a completely new town must have been overwhelming for Rosa, and since she'd struggled during her travels, he was sure she could use a good rest and a settling down period.

"I would love to see everything in detail, but I will admit that I could use a proper rest before seeing everything," Rosa admitted. "I am eager to see all of Bear Creek and meet everyone because I plan to make this town my home now, but I don't think I'll make the greatest impression on anyone if I'm dead on my feet." Jacob chuckled, thinking she'd already made a good impression on him. But he thought saying so would have been a little too forward at the moment. He found her charming and attractive and thought that their relationship was starting off on a good footing.

"Well, this is the inn," Jacob said as they came up to the large building. "Mr. and Mrs. Tibet host four rooms on the second floor and a large dining room below. Mrs. Tibet is a mighty fine cook so I know you'll be well fed while you're here. And most of the town folks dine here on a regular basis so I'm sure you'll meet everyone pretty quickly." Jacob led the way into a building that Rosa found quite charming. It was simply decorated, well maintained and tidy. These were good signs to Rosa since she'd been trained to have a critical eye when it came to the cleanliness of a house.

"Ah, there you are, Sheriff," came the voice of an elderly man as he approached them from the front counter. "And this must be Miss Casey whom we've heard so much about." Jacob chuckled nervously, hoping that Mr. Tibet wouldn't say anything too embarrassing or suggestive. He hadn't read any of Rosa's letters to anyone and he didn't want her to get the wrong impression.

"May I introduce you to Mr. Tibet, owner of the Bear Creek Inn," Jacob said as he let go of Rosa's arm now that they were inside. "I'm sure he could show you up to your room." Tanner was just coming down from a small hallway on the first floor and heading out the door to go gather the rest of Rosa's things. Jacob didn't know that there were rooms downstairs and was curious what Mr. Tibet had to say about the matter.

"Yes, I'd be happy to," Mr. Tibet said with a nod. "We put you at the end of the hallway here." He turned and pointed down the short hall-way. "Our apartment is just across the way. It is the room we always keep for anytime our children come to visit, and since Mrs. Tibet and I don't like the idea of you staying upstairs with all the miners, we wanted you to have the room."

"Oh, that is very kind of you," Rosa said with a smile. "I hope you didn't go to any trouble."

"No, no trouble at all," Mr. Tibet reassured her. Jacob felt relieved to know that Rosa would be staying closer to the other couple rather than being placed upstairs with the other guests. It would surely give Jacob peace of mind. "You can even come into the apartment and use the water closet any time you need to. Only place in town that has them." Mr. Tibet was proud of the fact since he knew that it was a very uncommon commodity. There was a second one on the top floor for all the guests to use, but he figured that since mostly men stayed at the inn it wouldn't be proper to have Rosa use it as well.

"Well, I look forward to my stay here at the inn," Rosa said honestly. She then turned to Jacob and said, "After I rest for a bit, perhaps we can continue that tour of the town."

"That sounds like a mighty fine idea," Jacob agreed. "I'll come back around supper time and we can have a bite to eat and I'll show you the sights."

"It's a deal then," Rosa said as she dipped her head. Then she followed Mr. Tibet across the main lobby towards the door. But she couldn't help looking over her shoulder as she watched Jacob leave the inn, thinking he was quite the handsome gentleman.

"Well, here you are," Mr. Tibet said as he opened the door for her. Rosa stepped inside, seeing that the room was nicely taken care of and well kept. She couldn't see a speck of dust even though the room had supposedly not been used for some time. A large stitch-work quilt hung on the end of the bed and Rosa thought it was the nicest quilt she'd ever seen, more elegant and detailed from what the factories in Boston could make.

"This looks lovely," Rosa said, turning to Mr. Tibet. He appeared to be eagerly waiting for her opinion. Just then, Tanner came in with the last of her things. She went to give him a few coins for his troubles, but he declined.

"Keep your money, Miss Casey. Though I appreciate the gesture," Tanner said as he nodded her way and then left the room.

"Well, I'll leave you to it," Mr. Tibet said as he went to shut the bedroom door. "Just let us know if you need anything. I'm usually at the counter or in the dining room, and you'll always find Mrs. Tibet in the kitchen." He gave her a kind smile before closing the door and allowing Rosa the privacy she desperately wanted.

Rosa looked at the large bed and thought she hadn't seen something so lovely in a long time. She had hardly slept well the last two weeks as she forced herself to sleep on a train without success. Rosa knew that she should have taken the time to unpack, but all she cared about was getting some proper rest.

After closing the curtains on the windows, Rosa undressed down to her undergarments and washed herself thoroughly from the basin of fresh water with a clean cloth that rested on a dresser. Then, she pulled on her last clean nightgown and got underneath the plush covers before laying her head down on a real down pillow. Rosa took a deep breath, thinking she could smell hints of lavender on the pillow case. She thought it was a nice touch, and that was the last thought she had before she quickly fell asleep.

CHAPTER 7

*J*acob was practically counting the minutes until supper time at the inn. He wanted to give Rosa plenty of time to rest after her travels, but he couldn't deny that he was eager to spend more time with her. Jacob thought that Rosa was very beautiful, but he wondered if that was only because he hadn't spent time with a single woman in a very long while. Perhaps back when he'd just turned sixteen. He hadn't realized how long it had been since he'd enjoyed the simple company of a single woman and he was now getting excited over the prospect of spending time with a fine woman such as Rosa promised to be.

A part of him did feel bad that she'd lost her cat while traveling and thought perhaps he could find her a new one. But when he reminded himself how much he disliked feline animals, he reasoned it wouldn't be a good idea. Part of him wanted to impress Rosa at any cost because he wasn't sure if he'd get an opportunity like this again. However, he also wanted to show her that he was considerate and not willing to sacrifice what he believed in just to please people. If he'd been that type of person, he wouldn't have made it this far as a sheriff.

Instead, Jacob did his best to stay busy while he waited. He stopped into the mercantile to talk with Mr. Fry to see if any mail had come for him on the stagecoach or if any telegram had come down the line.

"No, none of that has come in for you, Sheriff," Mr. Fry had said with a smile. "But I'd love to hear more about that young lady that came in on the coach." Jacob couldn't help but smirk as he shared some details with Mr. Fry about Rosa.

"If all things go well, I like to think I'll be a married man before too long," Jacob said, hoping to stay optimistic through this whole relationship. He knew that things weren't completely certain now that Rosa was in Bear Creek, but he still hoped that things would ultimately work out.

"Well, any woman that is willing to give you a shot at marriage is moving along on the right path," Mr. Fry said encouragingly. "Make sure to bring her by so I can introduce her to the missus."

"Sure thing, Mr. Fry," Jacob said in parting. He didn't need to do any shopping, but he browsed through the new selection of products anyways. Afterwards, he left the mercantile and made his way over to the Sheriff's Office, debating on whether or not he was going to change into something a little more comfortable. He didn't wear his official uniform that often and the monkey suit was a little tighter than he remembered. Thinking a change of wardrobe wouldn't hurt, he went into the Sheriff's Office and made his way up to his apartment so he could take his time changing. Even though he'd gotten used to using his left arm to change, he still had to be careful not to bump his right arm and the process took longer than he would have preferred.

"You up there, Jacob?" came a voice from down below. Jacob was a little surprised to hear the voice and hollered back down at the man.

"Is that you, Mathew?" Jacob asked as he pulled on his Western shirt.

"Yeah, I came in to get some feed from the livery stables for the horses. Thought I'd stop by and say hi," Mathew called back up.

"Alright, just give me a moment." Jacob tried to hurry up but found that he could only go so fast. Finally he made his way back down into the Sheriff's Office and gave Mathew the best hug he could with his left arm.

"Feels like I haven't seen you in ages," Jacob said as he took a good look at Mathew. He appeared as exhausted as Rosa had looked when she first got off the stagecoach and it made Jacob a little worried.

"Yeah, well. Being a parent is harder than anyone could ever tell you," Mathew said with a deep sigh. "But it's given me and Jenny more love than we ever thought possible." Jacob chuckled as he slapped Mathew on the back.

"Babies don't stay babies forever," Jacob said. "Hey, want to hear something pretty exciting?"

"Sure, I'm down for a good story," Mathew replied. Jacob leaned on his desk as he looked at his friend, a bright smile on his face.

"I put in a mail-order-bride ad," Jacob started with. He watched as Mathew's eyes grew large and a smile of his own crossed his face.

"Well, how about that," Mathew exclaimed. "Have you been writing any reply letters?"

"Not only that, but the woman I have been corresponding with just showed up in Bear Creek today." Jacob was getting a kick out of seeing how shocked he could make his friend.

"She's in town already? My word, you really have been keeping a tight lid on this one." Jacob shrugged his shoulders, the action still causing his right arm some pain. He grimaced as he tried to ignore the pain once more.

"I didn't want to go telling everyone about it just in case nothing worked out," Jacob explained. "You know how folks are around here."

"Do I ever." Mathew sighed as he rubbed his hands through his brown hair. It was starting to get long and shaggy again, and he was certain that the barber, Mitchel Franks, would get on Mathew before too long about looking decent again. "Dr. Harvey paid Jenny and me an unexpected visit this past week because someone in town said that little Michael was under the weather. The boy's been fine and dandy since the day he's been born."

"That really does sound like a bother." Jacob shifted his weight on the desk, knowing that people in town were always just trying to help. It was both a positive and a negative aspect of living in a remote country town.

"Well, that's enough about me. When do we get to meet this mysterious woman?" Mathew said.

"Rosa just got into town today and was a little worse for wear," Jacob admitted. "She's resting now at the inn. Mr. and Mrs. Tibet are letting her use the room downstairs. She might be able to become Mrs. Tibet's assistant in the kitchen. But I'll be going over to the inn this evening to have dinner with her."

"That's quite the development," Mathew said as he rubbed his chin. "Margret had mentioned something the other night about a woman coming into town to perhaps help out Mrs. Tibet. Never would have thought she'd be your mail-order-bride." They chuckled together as Jacob nodded in agreement.

"Well, I'm just willing to see how things go. She's a looker, that's for sure. But I get that there is more to a marriage than just two good looking people."

"There certainly is," Mathew said with a chuckle. "It's a lot of hard work, determination. But more than all of that, you really need to be sure you love the woman before you say, 'I do'."

"I appreciate the sound advice," Jacob said, wondering what he was going to do with the time on his hands.

"Well, Jacob, I best be off. I want to get home before it gets dark and make sure mama and baby are doing well," Mathew said as he made his way towards the door. "You make sure to bring Rosa out when you get a chance, even if I have to come into town and get you two."

"I appreciate the offer," Jacob said as he opened up the door for Mathew. "Riding isn't really possible right now, but I'm sure I could still drive a wagon if need be."

"Alright then. Take care." Jacob waved as Mathew left the Sheriff's Office. He was pleased to see his friend, but he was reminded once more of his limitations. He'd love to accept Mathew's offer and take

Rosa to go see the ranch and meet more people. But he wasn't sure if that would even be possible till he could start using his right hand again.

Jacob shut the door, trying not to have a sour mood. He was still excited that Rosa had finally made it into town and that this evening he was going to be spending time with her. He only hoped that his injured right arm didn't get in the way of them being able to have a real relationship.

AFTER HER LONG nap in an actual bed, Rosa felt like a completely new person. She didn't feel as sour or exhausted as when she first arrived in town. She chose to dress in one of her finer gowns, the one that Katelyn had insisted on buying for her in case she had a special event to attend. Considering the fact that she was about to have dinner for the first time with the man she'd traveled all this way to marry, she figured that now was as good a time as any to make a good impression on the Sheriff.

Rosa looked at herself in the small looking glass that hung on the wall over the dresser. She tilted her head back and forth, taking in her appearance. She had managed to put up her curly blonde hair into a fashionable arrangement, but she thought she would never really look as stunning as Katelyn often did after she'd finished with her hair.

"That's enough, Rosa," she said to herself in the mirror. "Stop comparing yourself to others." She nodded to herself and straightened her posture. She was here in Bear Creek to start her life over and make a good name for herself. And if all things worked out, she would be a married woman before too long. Then she could possibly have the large family she'd always dreamed of.

A knock on the door pulled Rosa from her thoughts. Wondering who it could possibly be, she turned from her reflection and walked over to the door. As she pulled it open, she smiled brightly as Jacob looked down on her, his bright blue eyes filled with warmth.

"Why hello there, Jacob," Rosa said opening the door wide. She stepped out into the hallway, knowing it would be improper to invite him into her room for a chat. Katelyn might have been that rebellious, but she certainly was not.

Jacob had to remind himself to breathe as he looked down at Rosa. She'd dressed in a satin gown made from layers of violet in different shades. Black lace trimmed the collar of the dress, as well as the puffy sleeves. She was a vision to behold and Jacob had to remind himself to speak when she started to giggle.

"Forgive me, Rosa. It's just been a very long time since I've had the pleasure of spending company with such a beautiful woman," Jacob admitted as a blush came to his cheeks. He normally wasn't this shy or stunned. He was the type of man anyone could rely on when things became chaotic. But here he was getting tongue-tied over a woman.

"Well, thank you for the compliment." Rosa lowered her eyes for a moment, thinking things were off to a good start.

"Let me show you to the dining room," Jacob offered as he moved to the side so Rosa could get by. The hallway was a bit narrow and he didn't want her to feel like she was getting blocked in.

"I certainly smell something wonderful." Rosa walked alongside Jacob, eager to spend the evening with this attractive, though slightly shy, man. "I'm not certain if I'll be familiar with the menu or the type of things that Mrs. Tibet likes to cook, but I've always been proficient about following exact orders."

"Must have come from your previous employment." Jacob showed her the way to the dining room, which was already starting to fill with patrons. Jacob wondered how fast the news about Rosa's arrival had spread through the town and how many of those dining at the inn tonight simply wanted to catch sight of the woman he hoped to marry.

"Mrs. Trevino was a very particular woman," Rosa explained as Jacob helped her into a chair. She liked to see that he had some gentle-manly qualities. It seemed that not all frontier men were rough around the edges. Jacob was proving to be quite the catch. And even though his right arm was in plaster, he still looked stunning in his Western shirt.

"I hope you had kind employers at least," Jacob said, wanting to keep this conversation going. He was very curious about Rosa and wanted to learn all he could about her.

"Yes, the Trevino family were very kind people. It's just that Mrs. Trevino liked things a very particular way." Rosa chuckled at the memory of Mrs. Weatherlore and her run-ins with the mistress of the house. "I often felt very bad for the housekeeper since she was the one in constant contact with Mrs. Trevino. I was lucky to have a charge as kind as Katelyn."

"In your letters you had mentioned that you had been with the family since you were twelve."

"That is true," Rosa said softly with a nod of her head. Her eyes wandered for a moment, the feeling of being lost in the world returning to her. She'd never really had a family even though the Trevino family had welcomed her into their home and provided her a place to live. She'd even been trained well so that one day she could honestly have any position she wanted within the households of the elite of Boston. A part of her had to be thankful for that.

Their conversation was interrupted as they were approached by Mr. Tibet. He came over with an older woman that Rosa could only assume was Mrs. Tibet. Rosa rose from her chair at once, wanting to make a good impression on her possible future employer.

"Oh, have a seat my dear," Mr. Tibet insisted. Rosa obliged as she sat once more. "Miss Casey, I'd like you to meet my amazing wife." Rosa looked at the older woman who was plump and stout. Mrs. Tibet had a bright smile and such warm brown eyes that she felt she could really enjoy being around her.

"It's a pleasure to meet you, Mrs. Tibet. I noticed your needle work in the bedroom. What a fine quilt you've made," Rosa said.

"My goodness, what fine manners," Mrs. Tibet replied. "It's hard to think that such a fine woman such as yourself would be an experienced cook." Rosa chuckled, knowing that the older woman was simply paying her a compliment.

"Rosa's been classically trained in housekeeping since she was twelve," Jacob spoke up, wanting Mr. and Mrs. Tibet to see what great value Rosa had. He smiled at Rosa then, hoping she didn't mind that he was speaking on her behalf.

"My goodness, you must have some fine stories to tell if you've been in service for that long," Mrs. Tibet said as Rosa laughed. She nodded, knowing that there were quite a few stories she could share with the older woman.

"I'm certain I could fill your ears for hours," Rosa assured her. "Though I was trained to be a lady's maid, I often enjoyed my time in the kitchen. It was part of my initial training that I learn to make my charge's favorite foods in case Cook was unable to."

"Well, around these parts, we all serve each other," Mr. Tibet said with a stern nod. Rosa didn't take offense, understanding that how people thought here in Bear Creek would be very different from those who lived in Boston and could afford almost every luxury.

"I'm pleased to hear so," Rosa said. "I think serving others is very important when wanting to support a strong community." Jacob couldn't feel more prouder in that moment as he looked at Rosa. She was not only talking for herself, but also being very logical. He was starting to think she would really have good potential in Bear Creek.

"Well, I better get back in there before people start to think I'm slacking," Mrs. Tibet said. "After dinner, I'd like to show you around the kitchen. Perhaps talk about what recipes we might both know?"

"I'd be delighted, Mrs. Tibet," Rosa replied. When Mrs. Tibet walked off, Mr. Tibet then gave them menus and asked what they'd like to enjoy that evening.

"What would you suggest?" Rosa asked Jacob. He looked up from his menu and peered at her, wondering what a woman from Boston might enjoy. Jacob knew that honesty was the best policy and figured he'd go with his gut feeling.

"Mrs. Tibet makes a mighty fine shepherd's pie," Jacob said. "Really, everything she makes is very delicious. But that seems to be many people's favorite."

"Well then, I think that's what I'll have." Rosa handed her menu back to Mr. Tibet and then finally she was left alone with Jacob.

"So, why don't you tell me about the bear incident and your arm," Rosa suggested. She wanted to learn more about Jacob and perhaps a bit about Bear Creek itself. Jacob didn't mind the question but would have rather listened to Rosa talk about herself. He was dying to learn if she would be the one for him.

"Well, I was headed up into the mountains to the west of town to meet up with Edward James. He's the man that bought the mine last year and has started hiring miners to work there," Jacob started with. "I was with my deputy, Tanner, when we crossed over the creek and immediately came upon a momma bear and her cubs. Before I could back up my horse, the bear stood up on her hind legs and spooked my horse. I got bucked off right into a pile of logs and boulders and injured my arm real good."

"But what about the bear?" Rosa asked, concerned about having a similar encounter.

"Tanner scared it off with a few shots from his pistol. I pretty much blacked out after that, but Tanner went to get help from the Sioux and that's how I got back to town to get checked out by Dr. Harvey."

"And people still go into the mountains? The mine is still functioning?" Rosa wasn't feeling very reassured by Jacob's story and was truly worried about bears now.

Sensing Rosa's fear, Jacob did his best to reassure her.

"Bears have been a part of this part of Montana since well before settlers started coming this way," he said. "Brown Bear, the Sioux chief, didn't get his name from just anywhere. But, even so, things are normally peaceful. As far as I know, there has never been a bear attack and they haven't been spotted in town. The people know to keep away from the part of the mountains that bears often frequent, and the Sioux Indians keep the population from growing too large."

Rosa tried to maintain a pleasant expression on her face. The last thing she wanted Jacob to think about her was that she was a coward.

After all, she traveled all this way on her own and seemed to have done a pretty decent job so far.

"Well, I simply hope that I don't have to experience what you went through," Rosa said as she reached forward and grasped her cup. She took a drink of the water, the cool water seeming to soothe her.

"The likelihood is very small." Jacob gave her a kind smile, thinking that there would be much that Rosa would need to get used to when it came to living in Bear Creek. "I can't think of a reason why you would need to ever go up into the mountains at all, unless you were going to visit with Edward or his sister Phoebe. Or even Brown Bear and his people."

"I'm certain then that I will not have to worry about bears since I'm bound to be sticking close to town," Rosa reasoned.

"I'd like to take you out to meet my best friend, Mathew, and his wife Jenny. They just had a baby boy and I haven't been out to see them since he was born," Jacob said as he remembered Mathew's invitation. "They live a bit out of town, but nowhere near the mountain." Rosa nodded, thinking it would be nice to meet some of Jacob's close friends.

"I would like that very much. But I don't have much practice with riding a horse or leading a carriage. I hadn't had a reason to do so in Boston."

"Well, I'm sure with some practice, I could teach you the basics," Jacob offered. "I haven't been riding much myself since the accident and have needed to rely on my deputy for a lot lately."

"Tanner seems to be a very reliable young man." Jacob nodded, thinking he had the best deputy in the world.

"He's a life saver, that's for sure."

Mr. Tibet then came out of the kitchen carrying their order. He set the food on the table and refilled their water before going off again. Rosa looked down at the shepherd's pie, seeing the familiar pie crust but noticing how it was filled with various vegetables and some sort of meat. It smelled heavenly, and the juices that came seeping out of it made Rosa's mouth water. As she took a small bite, she sighed deeply.

It had been such a long time since she'd had a decent cooked meal that she felt like she was in heaven as she ate the food.

Jacob watched Rosa carefully, wanting to know what her reaction would be to the simple meal. As Rosa closed her eyes for a moment as she chewed the food slowly, Jacob was certain she liked the taste of it. Perhaps, Jacob thought, he had taken Mrs. Tibet's cooking for granted. He was thankful to live in a place where someone was willing to cook for others. The food was always good and the price was affordable. And with his arm being currently unusable, he was grateful to be able to go somewhere to eat a good cooked meal.

"Just wait till you try one of her desserts," Jacob said between mouthfuls.

"My word, she bakes as well?" Rosa asked. "The dinner is so delicious that I can only imagine what her baked goods taste like." Jacob nodded as he thought about Mrs. Tibet's peach cobbler. It was always his favorite and he tried to manage to get a slice every time the older woman baked that particular sweet treat.

"We'll have to see what she's been making lately," Jacob suggested. "You'll have to leave room for some dessert."

"After traveling for two weeks without a decently cooked meal, I'm sure I could manage two dinners in one sitting." They chuckled together, but Jacob couldn't deny that he liked the idea of Rosa not being ashamed of eating plenty in front of him. He'd heard about how women back East always ate a dainty amount in order to impress a gentleman. Rosa surely seemed to be acting herself in front of him and hadn't shied away from eating.

After they'd finished their dinner, Jacob ordered two slices of the custard pie Mrs. Tibet had made that day. Rosa looked forward to the pie; she had refused to spend her income on sweet treats during her travels. She carried with her a considerable sum of money, partly her savings during her time with the Trevinos, partly the payment Mr. Trevino had given her in recompense of her service with the family and, finally, the considerable sum of money that Katelyn had insisted she take. Rosa had sewn the stash into the lining of one of her trunks.

She looked forward to depositing the money at the bank tomorrow, but for now focused on the good company she was enjoying.

"So besides being crossed by a bear, is there much excitement that happens in Bear Creek?" Rosa asked once their custard pie had arrived. Jacob smiled, thinking he'd like to put Rosa on the list of exciting things that had happened to Bear Creek.

"For the most part, this is a quiet place. There are the occasional criminals that try to come through town and prey on the weak. It's my job to deal with them. There was a skirmish between the miners and the Indians last year, but that was only because the miners were trying hard to impose upon the Sioux."

"Are there many skirmishes with the Indians?" Rosa asked, another fear coming to mind.

"No," Jacob said with surety. "Brown Bear and his people are very peaceful. I would trust them with my life and have done so in the past." Rosa watched Jacob carefully, looking at his face and into his blue eyes to make sure she could trust what he was saying to be true. She knew that he was a well-respected sheriff, that much she'd learned in just one day. But when it came to her own safety in such a remote place, she couldn't be too careful.

"I believe you, Jacob," Rosa said then. "It will just take me some time to get used to all this newness." Jacob nodded, understanding Rosa completely. He was feeling pleased with the idea that she trusted him, though.

"And since I won't be going anywhere with this broken arm, I'll be here the whole time to help you get settled," Jacob said, wanting to assure her that she wasn't alone in all of this. Rosa smiled at him, unable to contain herself. It was a very sweet gesture and it made Rosa think that Jacob had plenty of potential to be a good husband for her.

"Well, this has been quite a lovely dinner," Rosa said, thinking she'd like to spend some time with Mrs. Tibet before she lost her wits. There was something about Jacob that made her feel at ease. "I think I should go have a visit with Mrs. Tibet and see her at work." Rosa looked around the room, thinking that the dining room was quite full. Various couples sat at tables, some just drinking, as well as several miners who grouped around larger tables to enjoy a dinner.

"I'm sure she'd appreciate the company," Jacob said as he stood. He laid a bill on the table, confident that it would be more than enough to pay for the meal and show his appreciation to Mr. and Mrs. Tibet. He was thankful that they'd been willing to house Rosa in the room they tried to save for their children.

"I hope we can visit again soon," Rosa said as she stood as well, appreciating Jacob's kind gesture to pay for the meal. "Perhaps you can introduce me to some more of Bear Creek tomorrow."

"I'll stop by in the morning as long as nothing serious is happening at the Sheriff's Office," Jacob agreed. He was already looking forward to it, in fact.

"Well, have a good evening, Jacob," Rosa said as she dipped her head. It was such a habit for her to do that she didn't think twice about it. She only realized afterwards that she didn't need to do it to people that weren't her employer. It would take some time to break that habit.

"Good evening, Rosa," Jacob said as he tipped his hat to her and made his way towards the front of the inn. After giving Mr. Tibet his compliments on the meal, he left the inn greatly looking forward to returning in the morning.

Rosa felt like she was walking on clouds as she left the dining room in search of Mrs. Tibet. She had enjoyed her meal with Jacob and thought him both gentlemanly and very handsome. But since it was important that she secure proper employment, she needed to find the woman that supposedly could benefit from her help.

"Mrs. Tibet?" Rosa called as she walked through the double door that led to the grand kitchen. It wasn't anything like the one she was used in the Trevino home, it had none of the up-to-date equipment, but she reasoned that anyone could make do. It had one large wood-burning stove with six hot plates on top. That would be plenty of room to cook up several different dishes each day, and the oven looked wide enough to prepare bread and different baked goods as well as roasting meat. A large countertop filled the middle of the kitchen, providing plenty of space for meal preparation. Rosa spotted a walk-in pantry with various hanging herbs and dried meats. Rosa had the opportunity to use an ice-box in Boston and figured that people in Bear Creek had to go without that convenient appliance. She would need to research whether there was an ice house in which winter ice could be stored for summer use.

"I'm over here, my dear," Mrs. Tibet called from the corner of the kitchen. She was there plating a few more slices of the custard pie that was waiting to be served on the counter in the corner.

"I've come to offer my assistance and to see the kitchen for myself," Rosa explained. "This is a very impressive space."

"Why thank you," Mrs. Tibet said as she set the plates on the counter near the open door. Rosa stepped back as the door opened and Mr. Tibet popped in real fast to take the plates and deliver them. Then, Mrs. Tibet went on to her next task, checking the order slips for the ones she needed to fulfill next. Rosa simply watched for a little while, thinking that it was rather impressive that Mrs. Tibet had kept up with the demand of serving food to others for such a long time by herself. It seemed like exhausting work, yet she went about it while humming.

"How do you know what dishes to serve every day?" Rosa asked as Mrs. Tibet stirred a pot on the stove. As Rosa caught a glance of its contents, she guessed that it was some kind of soup or stew.

"Oh, it's a matter of what I feel up to cooking each day and what ingredients I have to work with," Mrs. Tibet explained. "My mother raised and fed seven children and plenty of extended family. I sure learned a lot from her since I was the oldest child."

"Wow, I can't even imagine what that is like." Rosa's eyes widened at the thought of growing up with that many siblings, and then being the oldest and having to care for them all. She reasoned that it would have been a lot of work, but having grown up without any sort of family, she'd happily have traded her life for something similar to what Mrs. Tibet had experienced.

"And with four of my own, it was easy enough to remain cooking for a good-sized group. Now, with all my children grown and moved away, I can't seem to stop cooking for so many. That's when we decided to open up the bottom floor of the inn into a serving place where people could come and get a decent meal."

"That's very kind of you," Rosa said, thinking that she was doing a great service for the town. Mrs. Tibet shrugged her shoulders as she continued to hum. She moved from the stew to a fresh loaf of bread as she began to cut it into almost perfect slices. Rosa could tell that the woman was very experienced. And even though she hadn't been classically trained the way Rosa had, the older woman had years of experience doing what she was doing now.

"I hope I can start helping you in the kitchen before too long," Rosa spoke up. She didn't want to interrupt the woman's train of thought, but she wanted to be forward with her hopes of securing employment for herself.

"I think that would be lovely, my dear," Mrs. Tibet said with an honest smile. "But you won't want to wear a beautiful gown such as that."

"No, I wouldn't dare to wear such a fine gown while working in the kitchen," Rosa laughed as she ran her fingers down her front, the feeling of satin still so unfamiliar to her. "I simply wanted to wear something nice."

"I don't blame you. Sheriff Benning is a fine young man," Mrs. Tibet said as she worked. "Tomorrow evening you can help me with the dinner meal. Then, we can go from there."

"Certainly, Mrs. Tibet," Rosa said. She was about to curtsy when she stopped herself. Rosa had to remind herself that she was no longer in Boston and that she didn't need to be so formal any longer. "I guess I'll retire for the evening, but you can count on me tomorrow."

"Very good, my dear. Rest well," Mrs. Tibet said and gave Rosa a parting look before turning her attention back to the food.

Rosa left the kitchen and made her way to her room. Once she was behind the closed door of the bedroom, she locked it and took a deep breath. Considering how the night had progressed, she had plenty to be grateful for. She took her time readying for bed, taking off her gown and making sure to hang it up in the wardrobe so it wouldn't wrinkle.

Once she was in a nightgown and had combed her hair out, she settled into bed. She wasn't particularly tired but knew that it would be a good idea for her to get some rest. Rosa was excited about tomorrow, about working with Mrs. Tibet, but also spending the morning with Jacob. After thinking about how things sat with her, Rosa had a good feeling about Bear Creek and creating a new life for herself there.

CHAPTER 8

$\mathcal{B}$y the time morning came, Jacob was eager to meet up with Rosa. He wanted to show her everything about Bear Creek and perhaps take her a bit out of town to see the surrounding countryside. But by the time Jacob had dressed and had made his way down into the office, Tanner was entering in a hurry.

"Hey, Jacob. You need to read this," Tanner said as he shoved a telegram into his left hand. Jacob shifted it in his grip so he could read it properly.

Sheriff Benning. Stop. Bank robbers in Junction City. Stop. Be on the lookout. Stop. Marshall.

Jacob clenched his jaw as he read the words. He hated to think that criminals like that could have gotten away, especially from a bigger town such as Junction City. And if the Marshal of Montana was sending him this telegram, that meant that trouble might be on the way to Bear Creek.

"Seems we have some work to do," Jacob said as he set the telegram down on his desk. "We'll start patrolling town and keeping an eye out for newcomers."

"You mean that *I* will start patrolling?" Tanner emphasized. "You can barely ride a horse, let alone wield a pistol. If you do suspect anything, you'll need backup at the very least." Jacob ground his teeth together as he did his best to keep his temper in check. Now wasn't the time to lose his composure. After all, he'd promised Rosa he'd come to visit with her this morning and show her the rest of the town.

"Fine. Keep a close eye on who is coming and going in town, especially people we don't recognize. I know Edward James has a lot of new fellas working for him and I've just been accepting all newcomers as miners looking for work."

"Let's just not jump to conclusions till we can get a good idea of who we should be worried about."

"I hear you, Tanner. I'll do my best to keep settled." Jacob ran the fingers of his left hand through his hair, trying to take a deep breath. He was trying not to get angry over the fact that his right arm was injured and that if criminals did come to Bear Creek that he wouldn't be at his best to defend the town. His worst fears were seeming to come true with this shocking telegram. Jacob silently prayed that whoever these bank robbers were that they would just skirt around Bear Creek.

"With the mine becoming so successful, I'm sure Mr. Fritz has had plenty of business at the bank. I'm going to go talk to him now and then we'll meet up back here this afternoon. Just keep your eyes sharp and your pistol ready."

"Sure thing, Boss." Tanner gave him a small smile before he left the Sheriff's Office. Jacob tried to rotate his shoulders, feeling how stiff they were from all the tension and stress he'd been feeling lately. If he hadn't had a prior engagement, he'd consider trying to pour himself a bath. But Jacob had work to do and a young lady to spend time with.

Grabbing his Stetson from the hook on the wall next to the door, he placed it firmly on his head and headed out of the office. After locking it behind him, he crossed over the road and made a beeline straight for the bank. As he did so, he couldn't help gazing around the whole town, or at least as far as he could see from this angle. Everyone he spied was a familiar face, whether it was Dan Mavis as he made his way to the town hall to conduct his school lessons for the day, or Mr. Fry coming out onto the front porch to prop up his 'open' sign on the front porch. Jacob waved to Mr. Fry with his left hand, the action gradually becoming more familiar. Jacob knew it was best to keep a pleasant demeanor because the last thing he wanted to do was spread panic throughout the town.

The bell rang over the door as Jacob stepped into the bank. Mr. Fritz was the wealthiest man in town and he kept a very luxurious business. The hardwood floors were polished so that Jacob hated walking on them with dirty boots. But since he knew that Mr. Fritz employed Margret and Jenny to come and clean the bank once a week, he thought that he might as well keep the two women in business as well.

"Good day, Sherriff," Mr. Fritz said as he came around from the back room in response to the bell ring as Jacob came in through the door.

Jacob approached the front counter. "Morning, Mr. Fritz," he said. Red velvet was embedded in the counter, giving it an elegant look and feel as Jacob came and leaned upon it with his good arm. "I wanted to have a quiet word with you and I'm glad to see things aren't busy this morning."

"Miners usually came running in with their finds in the afternoon," Mr. Fritz explained. He was a tall and rangy man with a hawk nose. But his bright blue eyes helped soften his naturally serious expression together with the fact that he was a man that smiled often and therefore seemed gentler than he might otherwise appear.

"I just got a telegram from the Marshall of Montana. He let me know that there was a bank robbing in Junction City and to be on the lookout for any suspicious activity."

Mr. Fritz whistled as he crossed his arms over his chest. "Well aren't you full of such good news."

Jacob couldn't help but chuckle at the comment as he shifted his weight from one foot to the other. With his broken arm, getting comfortable wasn't really something he could achieve anymore, however much he moved around, which he did often.

"I wanted to come by and warn you and see what kind of defense you have in here." Jacob looked around, already thinking of possible scenarios. The only door he saw was the front one, and since the bank was sandwiched between the barber shop and the mercantile, there were no side windows.

"Only one way in and out," Mr. Fritz said, pointing. Then he gave a wave to the back office as he explained, "The cash and gold is stored in the back in an American Steam Safe Company safe straight from New York City. Once a month I have my associate from Denver, Colorado come in to transfer the gold to a safe place."

"Sounds like you have a pretty good operation going on here. But what do you do when bank robbers try to get access to your vault?" That's when Mr. Fritz reached underneath the counter and pulled out a very shiny and new rifle Jacob had never seen before.

"Let me introduce you to the latest and greatest from the Winchester Repeating Arms Company," Mr. Fritz explained as he set the rifle down on the counter and lightly ran his fingers up it. "It's a lever-action shotgun designed by John Browning himself. My associate brought this for me two months ago when I told him how busy things had gotten. It's locked and loaded, all ready for use."

"Mr. Fritz, you are just full of surprises today." Jacob marveled at the weapon, wondering how this modern weapon worked. "How does it handle?"

"It kicks a punch, that's for sure. But when it comes to fast and easy, this is the way to go."

"Seems like I need to update my personal collection once this arm heals." Jacob watched then as Mr. Fritz picked up the weapon and placed it back underneath the counter.

"How's the arm doing, Sheriff? Think you'll be back in action before too long?"

"Dr. Harvey explained that it will take several months for it to heal completely, though I should lose the plaster before then. I'll see how the trigger finger is working after that." Jacob tried to keep the grimace from his face as the thought of never being able to fire a pistol again crossed his mind. That was just a reality he wasn't ready to face, ever. Jacob was a proud sheriff and always wanted to protect Bear Creek.

"Well, I'll be praying for you for sure," Mr. Fritz said with a nod. "Wouldn't want any other man to be Sheriff of this town."

"That's the goal." Jacob pushed off the counter and peered around one last time, finally feeling confident that Mr. Fritz would be able to protect himself in case of a bank robbery. "Keep your eyes peeled for any suspicious people coming in. And I'll keep you posted if I learn anything else."

"Thank you, Sheriff. You have a good day now." Mr. Fritz then returned to his back office after Jacob had tipped his hat to him. Jacob made his way out of the bank feeling a little more confident than he had before. Now, all he had left to do for the morning was pay a very pretty lady a visit.

THE CALL of a rooster woke Rosa from a dead sleep. She opened her eyes, her mind racing to remember where she was. As she looked at the unfamiliar white-washed walls, the burgundy curtains over the windows, she reminded herself she was no longer in Boston nor traveling on a noisy train. Rosa sat up and pushed her curly blonde hair out of her eyes. She forced herself to take a long deep breath. The morning was early, but she was safe and sound at the inn.

As Rosa moved from the bed, she made sure to turn down the gingham quilt like she had done a hundred times before as a lady's maid. She had not only been responsible for keeping Katelyn's room tidy, but also her own living space. She fluffed the two pillows as well before she turned her attention upon herself.

Rising early wasn't a new ideology for Rosa. She'd been accustomed to rising early every day for her morning tasks. But now that she didn't have a set agenda or was expected to be anywhere at any certain time, Rosa almost felt at a loss. She had no idea what she should be doing with herself. She washed and dressed in one of the simple gowns she and Katelyn had decided were suitable for working days. She looked at the three trunks that Deputy Tanner had carried in and decided to unpack at least the one that held her day-to-day wardrobe. There was a chest of drawers that she soon filled. Then she made the bed and looked around. the room to see if there was anything else she could attend to.

Nothing needed pressed or mending, and everything looked to be in its proper order. Rosa took a deep breath then and tried to clear her mind. She was able to create any future she saw fit. She simply needed to let go of old habits. It would take some time since she'd been serving others since she was twelve. Now the only person she was responsible for was herself. It was a type of freedom she'd never experienced before.

Rosa left the room thinking that breakfast would be a good way to start the day. She expected Jacob to pay her a visit in the course of the morning and figured she should be ready to greet him. The inn sounded quiet as she went down the hallway. It was a bit dim since it was still so early in the morning. As she made her way into the kitchen, she was instantly greeted by the warmth of the stove as Mrs. Tibet stood feeding the fire within.

"Good morning, Mrs. Tibet," Rosa said with a smile. She hadn't expected anyone else to be up this early and was pleased to see a familiar face.

"Ah, good morning, Miss Casey. I hope I didn't wake you?" Mrs. Tibet said as she closed the oven door and turned to greet her.

"No, you did not. However, a very eager rooster did." Mrs. Tibet chuckled as she wiped her hands on her apron. Her long graying hair was tucked back into a bun, the hairstyle very familiar to Rosa. She'd only pinned back her golden curls, liking the freedom to style her hair anyway she saw fit.

"There is a small chicken coop behind the inn. It's where I get all my eggs. When the rooster crows, I'm up and at it."

"That's how life in Boston was for me." Rosa came around the corner and stood near the older woman as she watched her work. She was mixing familiar ingredients in a large bowl. Eggs, milk, and flour went in it and warmed water and yeast sat next to it in a small bowl. Then, Mrs. Tibet started to mix it all together with the ease of someone following a routine she'd done a hundred times before.

"I've never been anywhere but Bear Creek," Mrs. Tibet spoke up as she placed a towel over the mixing bowl once the ingredients had all been incorporated. If Rosa had to guess, she would say that the mixture would be set to rise before being made into loaves of bread. "Mr. Tibet and I settled here when we were young and the mine was just being discovered. We wanted to capitalize on this growing town and raise our children here."

"Sounds like Bear Creek is a nice place to raise a family if you and Mr. Tibet are still here."

Mrs. Tibet nodded as she pulled down a large cast iron skillet. "Raised four children without any issues. Even with managing this inn."

Mrs. Tibet removed one of the pot covers from the black stove and set the skillet on top of it. When she added the lard to the pan from a bowl that had been kept covered near the stove, it sizzled instantly. With the pan plenty hot and ready for cooking, Mrs. Tibet then started to crack eggs over it from a basket that had been sitting on the counter. Rosa watched the woman working with excellent speed and experience. The eggshells were tossed into the waste basket near the back door before she began to stir the pan of eggs, making them fluffy.

"I hope you're hungry," Mrs. Tibet spoke up. "I've never really been able to cook a small meal."

"I'm famished," Rosa spoke honestly. "Can I help prepare anything else to go with the eggs?"

"There's some day-old bread in the keeper over there." Mrs. Tibet turned and pointed to the other side of the kitchen with her wooden spoon. Rosa went over to the small wooden box and opened it to reveal the bread that had been prepared yesterday. "Slice it and I'll toast it once the eggs are done." Rosa pulled the loaf out of the box and shut the lid once more before returning to the center counter. It took her a moment to locate the bread knife in a drawer but she set about slicing the bread as Mrs. Tibet finished the eggs.

Mr. Tibet came in through the back door carrying a pail of milk about the time Mrs. Tibet had finished the eggs and was toasting the bread slices in the skillet. He set the pail down on the center counter and nodded to Rosa with a smile before turning to his wife.

"Mrs. Dillon sends her greetings," he said as he pecked a kiss onto his wife's cheek. He then took the pail and placed it inside the cool closet. It was a small closet, dark and close to the ground. Rosa watched with curiosity because she was used to having an ice chest available to keep fresh milk cool. Instead, this seemed to do the same job.

"How are the Dillons doing? Heard their little boy is under the weather," Mrs. Tibet asked.

"Marcus seems to be doing okay. He was in the field with the others. He milked Bessy all by himself today." Mrs. Tibet chuckled as she started to place the toasted bread on a serving plate on the center counter.

"Well, I guess you can't always believe what you hear. Just the other day someone said that little Michael had fallen ill, and Dr. Harvey went all the way out to the Jenkins' to find them all well."

"It's a small town, my dear." Mr. Tibet shrugged his shoulders as he pulled down a stack of plates from a cupboard and set them on the center counter. He handed one to Rosa before fixing himself his own plate. By the time Rosa had filled her plate with fluffy hot eggs and toast, several miners had started to come into the kitchen.

"Good morning, Mrs. Tibet. Mr. Tibet," came the cheerful voices of the miners. Rosa wasn't sure what to do so she took her plate and moved over to the other side of the kitchen.

"Ah, good morning, boys," Mrs. Tibet said cheerfully, as though she was greeting her own children. Rosa watched with a smile on her lips as Mrs. and Mr. Tibet fussed over their guests, making sure they had enough to eat before heading out to the mines. To Rosa it seemed as though Mr. and Mrs. Tibet never stopped being the dutiful parents they'd always been.

The inn guests came in and left in a hurry, grabbing a few pieces of toast and some eggs before heading out. Rosa imagined this is what it was like to take care of a large family. Rising early, making breakfast, making sure everyone had plenty to eat before heading off, either to school or work. Mornings at the Trevino home usually were a solitary affair since she rose early, took care of her duties, and ate bites of food between chores. Actually having a meal as a family wasn't a concept she was familiar with. It was certainly something she wanted to experience for herself one day.

As Rosa was helping Mrs. Tibet clean up the kitchen by placing all the dirty dishes in the dry sink, Mr. Tibet went out back to fetch water from the well. Rosa was in the middle of helping clean the dishes when a knock came to the kitchen door.

"Now who would that be?" Mrs. Tibet wondered as she dried her hands on her apron. She went over to the push-through door that led to the inn's main dining area and opened it to reveal Jacob standing on the other side. Rosa couldn't contain a smile as she finished washing the plate in her hand and set it on the towel next to the sink before drying her own hands.

"Sheriff, you know you never have to knock," Mrs. Tibet said with her hands on her hips.

"I know, Mrs. Tibet. But my mama taught me manners and I intend to use them." Mrs. Tibet chuckled as she shooed at him with her hand before moving onto her next task for the morning. She checked to see how her bread was rising before turning to the pantry. It gave Rosa the opportunity to approach Jacob without feeling as though she was going to be watched by the older woman.

"Good morning, Jacob," Rosa said with a kind smile. "You just missed breakfast."

"No problem. I've already had my morning coffee." Jacob smiled down at her, his bright blue eyes doing something to Rosa that no other man had been able to do in the past. She blushed, finding the feeling foreign.

"In that case, how about that official tour of Bear Creek?" Rosa figured it would be good to be out and about if she was going to be working in the kitchen with Mrs. Tibet. Though there was a beautiful, large window over the dry sink, the view was only of the backyard with the chickens.

"That's why I came by." Jacob then turned to Mrs. Tibet and asked, "You don't mind if I borrow your new assistant for the morning?"

"Oh, you two go have fun. I've managed this long on my own that I'm certain I could do for a morning." Mrs. Tibet then shooed them out of the kitchen just as Mr. Tibet was returning with a pail of fresh water for the dishes. Rosa had never really taken leisurely time for herself when she was a lady's maid. It felt a bit strange to leave a chore undone. She had to remind herself once more that she had much more freedom on her own and could spend the morning exploring the town.

Rosa followed Jacob out of the kitchen. At the front door of the inn, Jacob held the door open for her. As she stepped outside, the warm spring air greeted her, giving hints of a fast approaching summer. Rosa took a deep breath of the fresh air and thought how lovely it all was. No commotion of the city came to her ears as she walked with Jacob up the boardwalk. There were plenty of people milling about, but it wasn't loud and noisy as people shouted over each other or carriages thundered down the road.

"I can't believe how peaceful it is here," Rosa commented as she looked around at the shops.

"For the most part, yes," Jacob replied. "It's a bustle in the morning and afternoon, but compared to Boston, I'm sure it's a big change."

"But in a good way," Rosa said reassuringly. "Bear Creek might be a remote frontier town with not as many resources as Boston, but I think that is a positive thing."

"Well, there are all the necessities here. The town hall building over there serves as both the church and the schoolhouse. Dan Mavis is the schoolteacher, while Pastor Munster comes at least once a month to give a sermon on a Sunday." Rosa saw where Jacob was pointing and looked at the tall central building of the town. It had a bell tower at the top and two double doors for the entrance. A small set of stairs led up to the front doors. One hung open and Rosa could hear the excited chatter of children, making her think that a school lesson must be in session. The happy laughter made Rosa think of her own longing to have children.

"Next to the town hall there is the clinic where you'll often find Dr. Harvey during the day. On the other side of the street on the road heading out of town is where the Sheriff's Office is. That's where you'll find me most of the time since my apartment is over the office." Jacob pointed to all the buildings and Rosa paid attention, wanting to become as familiar with everything as soon as possible. The idea of Jacob living so close to the inn made Rosa realize just how often she was bound to run into him as she became settled in Bear Creek. It was certainly a positive of living in such a small town.

"On the other side of the town hall is a small boarding house that Mr. Cricket manages. They house most of the miners that work for Mr. James, but all of them would tell you that they'd rather stay at the inn." Rosa chuckled, thinking that it would be positively true since Mr. and Mrs. Tibet were such friendly hosts.

"It's not a place a young lady such as yourself should ever go into. It's just for men, and well, men will be men," Jacob warned. The last thing he wanted was for Rosa to get caught up into some trouble because a needy miner would consider her easy prey. He knew what type of things went on at the boarding house and he wanted to make sure Rosa understood it wasn't any place for a woman. Even as he looked at the boarding house, he saw standing in the open front door that frowsy doxy who came in on the same stagecoach as Rosa. She was coughing badly and retreated into the building, closing the door after her. Jacob frowned. Something told him that she and the other one who'd arrived two days ago were trouble.

"I'll make sure to avoid it at all costs then." Rosa wasn't looking for any male company and would rather enjoy walking with Jacob through town than peeking into a place she shouldn't be in. She'd caught a glimpse of that woman who had made her coach trip such a nightmare and was relieved when she went inside.

"But there is a butcher shop across from it," said Jacob, pointing. "I'm sure if Mrs. Tibet sends you out for errands, it will either be to the mercantile or the butcher shop. Mr. Tibet tends to visit the dairy farmer in the morning for milk and such."

"Seems like you know what everyone does in the town," Rosa

observed. Jacob chuckled as he nodded, understanding from Rosa's perspective that might seem a little intrusive.

"It's part of my job as Sheriff to understand what is going on in town. I have many of the daily habits of the locals here in town memorized so that if anyone did go missing or something is wrong, I can start with where I know they should be." Rosa thought about that and could see the logic behind Jacob's approach.

"And no one thinks you're snooping on them or anything?" she said.

Jacob laughed then, finding her words very refreshing. He'd never thought of what he did as snooping.

"Well, I don't go sharing everyone's business with the others in town, so as long as I'm keeping everyone safe, I don't consider it snooping," Jacob explained once he got control over his mirth. The sound of his laughter was pleasing to Rosa and she imagined listening to the sound of it throughout the day. She forced herself to get control over her thoughts and emotions as they passed by the barbershop and made it back to the mercantile.

"Care if we go in so I can take a quick look around? I'm curious to see what things are kept in stock."

"Certainly," Jacob said as he held open the door for her. "I'm certain Mr. Fry is eager to meet you." Rosa thought that statement was understated for as soon as she stepped inside, the man was quick to come around the counter and greet her.

"Good day to you. My name's Joseph Fry and my wife, Francine, is in the back with the mending," Mr. Fry said as he came forward and shook Rosa's hand with enthusiasm. Rosa did her best to keep her composure because she'd never been so excitedly greeted before. Made her think that newcomers didn't make their way to Bear Creek that often.

"It's a pleasure to make your acquaintance, Mr. Fry," Rosa said as she withdrew her hand from his, thinking the older man could shake it all day.

"My, my, what pretty manners you have," Mr. Fry remarked. "Is there anything I can help you find?"

"No, I'm just browsing today. Jacob is being kind enough to show me around town this morning."

"Well, it might not be very large, but we make do with what we have."

"How's Mrs. Fry doing today?" Jacob asked, hoping to draw Mr. Fry's attention to him so Rosa could have a moment of peace. She smiled at him as Mr. Fry started to chatter away. She then turned her gaze towards the dry goods and started to wander up and down the two aisles. Rosa was able to find a good number of basic items from flour and sugar, to plain fabrics and yarn. Many of the items were unfamiliar to Rosa and she figured that the products available for purchase must be as different as living in a remote town for the first time was.

Rosa reminded herself not to become discouraged. It would take time to learn the proper way of doing things in Bear Creek. She lifted her eyes from the shelving of jarred vegetables and saw how Jacob was keeping Mr. Fry occupied with their conversation. Though it seemed that it was the shop keeper who was doing all the talking. But it gave Rosa the opportunity to really look at Jacob. She took in his strong jaw, combed-over sandy-blond hair and those bright blue eyes. Even though his right arm was held in a sling, the way his Western shirt hugged his frame suggested he was well muscled. All in all, Jacob Benning was an attractive man and Rosa figured she was lucky that the Sheriff hadn't turned out to be unappealing.

When Jacob glanced over at Rosa, she quickly looked away, trying to appear as if she was interested in the jarred vegetables as she picked up one full of carrots and turned it around in her hands. A blush came to her cheeks as she hoped that Jacob didn't think she was staring at him.

Jacob's years of working as a law enforcer kicked in when he felt someone watching him. He'd looked over to Rosa to see her eyes locked on him, seeming to detail his every characteristic. Jacob certainly didn't mind having her attention on him and couldn't contain the smirk that came across his lips as she quickly looked away. It was the deep blush that settled on her face that gave her away.

Jacob returned his attention back to Mr. Fry, who could always talk the day away. It was the perfect cover for keeping an eye on Rosa without her noticing his ever-watchful eyes. Even though she wore a simple day gown that was nothing compared to the gown she had worn last night, Jacob still found her to be very pretty.

"Did you know that most of the miners have fallen ill?" Mr. Fry said, causing Jacob's attention to be pulled back to the store owner.

"Fallen ill? You sure about that? I've heard a lot of false stories about illness lately."

"No, I mean it this time. One of those fellas that stay at the boarding house came in this morning wanting something for his cough."

"Miners coughing isn't uncommon for their line of work. The mountain dust might be getting to them and they just need some fresh air."

"No, this guy had a runny nose too and blood-shot eyes." Jacob didn't like the sound of this. In a small town, disease could run rampant and affect everyone very quickly. With only one town doctor, a simple cold being passed around could easily lead to a pandemic.

"If I tell Dr. Harvey, I'm letting him know you told me first," Jacob reasoned. "But I'll go stop by the clinic after a bit."

"Wouldn't hurt to let the good doctor know." Mr. Fry turned then as Rosa rejoined them. "Find everything to your liking?"

"You have a very nice store, Mr. Fry. I'm sure to find all my needs met here." Rosa glanced at Jacob then and thought that statement could go further than just complimenting Mr. Fry on his mercantile.

"Well, you just let me and the missus know if you need anything specific. I keep a few catalogues behind the counter when something special needs to be ordered in. Special occasion stuff and all of that." Mr. Fry winked at Jacob before returning back behind the counter. Rosa couldn't contain her smile as she understood the context of the man's words. It was a small town, after all, and it wouldn't take long before everyone understood the initial reason why Rosa had come to live in Bear Creek. The idea didn't embarrass her at all, but only made her more willing to meet everyone in town. Which reminded her. "I think it's time I returned to helping Mrs. Tibet in the kitchen," she said, smiling at Jacob. "I have so enjoyed seeing Bear Creek. Perhaps we can meet again this evening?"

When those brown eyes smiled into his, Jacob would have been willing to do anything for Rosa.

"How about I show you over to the clinic? I have a message to deliver to Dr. Harvey," Jacob offered as he held the door open for Rosa as they walked out onto the front porch.

"I'd be willing to join you," Rosa agreed. They crossed the road together after two men on horses came riding through the center of town. Jacob nodded towards them, recognizing the two cattle hands that Mathew had hired last year. He wasn't certain why they were heading in and perhaps were just running errands for the family. Right now, Jacob was focused on letting Dr. Harvey know of a possible situation over at the boarding house.

"Dr. Harvey has been in town ever since the first ranchers came out this way. Delivered me and most of the people in town." Rosa looked at Jacob, a bit surprised. She assumed that Dr. Harvey must be a much older man then. They crossed the street together, and once they approached the door to the clinic, Jacob held it open for her. Rosa liked the gentleman-like characteristic and figured she could get used to a man treating her with respect.

As Rosa stepped inside the clinic, she was immediately taken back. The lobby seemed to be full of men as they coughed into their hands or elbows. An older man came hurrying from the back room, and as Rosa made eye contact with the very concerned gentleman, she had a feeling of great concern pass through her.

"Jacob, get the woman out of her. I'm dealing with a rapidly spreading sickness in here," said the older man as he started passing vials of some clear liquid out to all the men that stood close together. Rosa took several steps back until she was out of the room. It smelled of musk and dirt, and she wondered what had made all these men so sick as they continued to cough hard and loudly.

Jacob reached out and pulled Rosa towards him before quickly shutting the door with his boot. He hadn't been expecting to walk in on such a scene and thought that what Mr. Fry had to say warranted plenty of truth. Jacob quickly shut the door, stunned by the number of miners who seemed to have been affected so far.

"What do you think has happened?" Rosa asked as she looked up at Jacob. He was still holding her arm, pulling her close to his body. She didn't really think about their closeness till then, as her mind continued to replay what she'd just seen.

"Mr. Fry had told me one of the miners that is staying at the boarding house had come into the mercantile looking for something to ease his cough. I was heading over here to let Dr. Harvey know, but it seems like he already does."

Jacob looked down at Rosa, realizing he was still holding onto her with his left hand. He slowly let go of her arm and took a step back, giving Rosa a sheepish grin. He hadn't realized that he'd been holding onto her so tightly. It had been a sudden reaction the moment she'd stepped inside the clinic and they were faced with that terrible scene of immense sickness.

"Seems we should be moving on then," Rosa said as she glanced back at the closed door. She could still hear the coughing of the many miners inside and wondered what could be causing such a thing to happen to so many people. She'd heard about miner's cough before, but all the miners that were staying at the inn seemed fine enough this morning.

"I agree. Let's get you back over to the inn." Jacob led Rosa back over to the inn as his mind started to race. He wanted to get Dr. Harvey's opinion on what was happening to the miners and see if he needed to have a talk to Edward James about anyone else that might have fallen ill.

"I appreciate the time you took out of your morning to show me the town." Rosa's voice cut through Jacob's thoughts as they walked together. He smiled at her, thinking the time they'd spent together that morning was going to be the highlight of his day.

"It was my pleasure." When they reached the inn, Jacob held the door open for her, wishing they still had more time to spend together and really get to know one another. "Please let Mr. and Mrs. Tibet know I appreciate everything they are doing for you."

"I'll make sure to do so, yes," Rosa said in parting. Feeling a little brave, she turned and looked over her shoulder at Jacob as she said, "Don't be a stranger now." The smile that lit up Jacob's face told Rosa all that she needed to know. She felt proud of herself for daring to be a bit flirtatious as she made her way to the kitchen. She heard the front door close behind her and smiled to herself, already eager to spend time with Jacob once more.

CHAPTER 9

*B*y the time dinner time had come around, Rosa was deep in her work in the kitchen. After Mrs. Tibet had explained what she wanted to start cooking that day, Rosa was quick to put on her apron and lend a hand. It felt good to have something to busy herself with, and once Mrs. Tibet explained how to prepare each dish, Rosa found it to be simple enough work.

On the menu for that evening was going to be two beef roasts that Mr. Tibet had picked up from the butcher. They would be braised in the oven for a few hours and served with a medley of vegetables from potatoes to carrots. Mrs. Tibet said that the potatoes were part of the harvest from last year and soon other common vegetables would be used from the garden such as beets, celery, Brussels sprouts, corn, and all manner of beans.

The biggest thing that Rosa was quick to learn is that any food that was going to be prepared had to be locally grown or harvested some way. In Boston, Rosa was so used to going to the local market and getting anything she needed if she was preparing something special for Katelyn or running errands for Cook. But in Bear Creek, resources had to be shared. Mr. Tibet helped run errands in the morning to gather what Mrs. Tibet would need for the day. Vegetables from last year's garden were kept in a root cellar, while other things were either pickled or salted to preserve. It was all a big learning experience for Rosa that she continued to learn about as she aided Mrs. Tibet.

"Make sure there is plenty of water in the roasting pots before we stick them in the oven or they'll dry out," Mrs. Tibet instructed as Rosa stood at the center counter with both roasts. She'd just placed them in the pots and was beginning to salt them when she had received the instruction from Mrs. Tibet. Having been used to modern plumping, Rosa had to remind herself that the water came from a well and that she needed to fetch the water before adding it to the pots. There were two water closets in the inn, but water hadn't been piped to the kitchen, making the work take a bit longer than Rosa would have first imagined.

"Then cut up the onions and garlic. Those will go around each roast to help with the flavor and to keep the moisture in," Mrs. Tibet instructed next. She was currently rolling out five loaves of bread that would go into the oven with the roasts. She had plans to make a cherry pie with the preserves she had left and even considered making a second since she had help in the kitchen. Mrs. Tibet saw that Rosa was not only good at listening to her instructions, but obviously had skills when it came to working in a kitchen. She thought that she would make a good wife for any of the many gentlemen in town and wondered how her relationship with the Sheriff would turn out as the days continued.

"Is this enough, Mrs. Tibet?" Rosa asked once she had finished the dreadful work of cutting up all the onions. She used her apron to wipe the tears out of her eyes, never having enjoyed cutting up onions even though it always made food taste even better.

"Yes, dear," Mrs. Tibet said with a chuckle. "Go wash your hands and splash some cool water onto your face. That will get the onion smell out of your eyes." Rosa only nodded as she went over to the dry sink and used a pail of water to wash up. She sneezed a few times as she did so, thinking that the combination of garlic and onion had really gotten to her.

"Bless you," Mrs. Tibet said as Rosa continued to sneeze.

"Thank you," Rosa said right before she blew her nose on her handkerchief and replaced it into her apron pocket. "Those are some strong onions." Mrs. Tibet chuckled as she finished kneading the dough and started to place the loaves in the pans. As Rosa finished up the roasts, she carefully placed the lids on and carried them one by one to the oven. As Mrs. Tibet opened the oven door, Rosa slid in the pots after making sure the fire was still burning strong. With an iron prong, she moved the coals around the pots to make sure that every-thing cooked evenly. Then, she helped put the loaves of bread in the hottest part of the oven and close to the door so they could be pulled out before the roasts would be finished in the afternoon.

"You'll have to excuse me, Mrs. Tibet. I need a breath of fresh air," Rosa said as she fanned herself with her hand. The heat from the oven made her feel like she was having a hot flash and she desperately wanted to step outside a moment. Mrs. Tibet shooed her out, a look of concern on her face as Rosa quickly opened up the back door and stepped out into the afternoon sun.

The shade behind the inn helped cool Rosa as she continued to fan herself with her apron. She took several deep, long breaths to help flush the heat off her skin. She'd never really felt this hot before when working in the kitchen. Only when the days became hot in the summer that the oven was unused and replaced with other cool options such as sandwiches and cold soup.

"You alright, Miss Casey?" Mrs. Tibet said as she came to the back door. Rosa nodded as she continued to fan herself.

"Just needed some fresh air. Feels like it's a hot summer's day in there." Mrs. Tibet looked at her with much concern, thinking that it felt comfortable enough in the kitchen. The older woman wondered if she was simply used to the warmth of the kitchen and that perhaps Rosa would have to become accustomed to it over time. But as she continued to watch Rosa struggle with cooling herself, she wondered if the young lady wasn't feeling very well.

"Things get busy around four in the afternoon. Why don't you go rest for a spell and meet me back in the kitchen then to help serve up the orders?" Mrs. Tibet suggested as she coaxed Rosa back inside. Rosa nodded as she gave the woman a weak smile. The idea sounded fine enough as she started to want to strip out of her many layers. She was wearing three petticoats underneath her day gown since she was used to wearing them while serving in the Trevino family, but was thinking that they would not be so convenient in the West.

Rosa made her way out of the kitchen and hurried to her room. Once behind the closed and locked door of her bedroom, she pulled off her apron and set it on the edge of the bed before stripping out of her clothes. Once she was down to her slip, she went over to the water basin and began to bathe herself, the cool water feeling refreshing on her skin.

Rosa glanced at her reflection in the looking glass, surprised by how pale her skin had become. She leaned forward, needing a closer look as she stared at her eyes and saw that they had become red. Rosa sighed deeply as she turned to her bed and got under the covers. She figured that she had some allergies to the new environment and just needed some rest. After all, she'd just arrived into town yesterday and was most likely still fatigued. It didn't take Rosa that long to fall asleep after she laid her head down on the cool pillow. When the time came to rise again and help Mrs. Tibet in the kitchen, Rosa felt worse. She started coughing, hard, barking coughs and felt as though she was burning up. Mrs. Tibet brought her a cup of tea, took one look at her new helper and told her to stay in bed. "It seems as if you picked up some infection from your journey."

Rosa thought of the woman she'd been jammed next to in the stagecoach.

When Jacob came by that evening, Mrs. Tibet told him the bad news. "No, I don't think you can see her," she said. "It'll be something she picked up on her journey. If she's no better tomorrow morning, I'll send for the doc."

Jacob went back to his office with a sick feeling in his heart. It had never occurred to him that his wooing could be interfered with by a fever. Infections out here were the very devil. The medicines that the doctor had available were limited to dealing with common complaints.

~

LATER THE NEXT DAY, Jacob sat in the Sheriff's Office with both Tanner and Dr Harvey. He felt as though his world had been flipped upside down. The older man looked exhausted as he related his story.

"I have six men in the clinic who can't seem to catch their breaths. At first, I just thought it was miner's cough, but they're all snotty with runny noses and bloodshot eyes," Dr. Harvey explained. "I've given them all doses of laudanum to help them get some rest. But since they are all from the boarding house, I have a suspicion that there might be more of them before too long."

Jacob sure didn't like the sound of that. Yesterday it had been news of bank robbers in the territory. Now he had to worry about what was making all these miners so sick. He knew he needed to get over to the boarding house and see what was going on, but he also needed to keep an eye out for suspicious newcomers.

"Doc, what do you plan to do with them? How can you treat their sickness?" Jacob asked. He hoped the doctor had some sort of cure before too many people got sick.

"Mitchel Franks is coming over to the clinic in a bit to do the bloodletting. I have to go check with Mr. Cricket to see if anyone else is sick and get them over to the clinic before they can pass on the illness. My hope is that they can just ride it out, but there isn't really more I can do besides make them comfortable."

Jacob ran his hand through his hair as he looked at Tanner. The deputy was a few years younger than him but had plenty of experience working with Jacob. But they had never really faced a problem like this before. How could they keep the town safe from something like an illness?

"Tanner, head over to the town hall as quietly as you can and let the Mayor know what's going on. I don't want people panicking or starting rumors. Doc, are these men going to be okay? Is it just some bad cold?"

"Jacob, it's late spring. Normally I would just say they have spring allergies to everything growing and blooming, but these men have signs of a chest cold by the way they're trying to hack up whatever's in their lungs."

"Is there any chance this sickness could kill people?"

Dr. Harvey went quiet then, a grim expression on his face. "There is no telling what's going to happen, but the likelihood is always there when people get this sick," he explained. Jacob was instantly taken back by the news. He would have never dreamed that a sickness could start wiping people out.

"Well, let's not jump to any conclusions just yet," Jacob suggested. "I'll come with you to the boarding house and we can see what's going on first." Dr. Harvey simply nodded as Tanner opened up the door for them. They all filed out of the Sheriff's Office, Jacob taking a moment to lock the door before following the doctor down the road to the boarding house. He looked over his shoulder and watched as Tanner made his way to town hall. The deputy smiled at those he passed by on the street and Jacob was proud of the man for keeping his composure even though he was about to go deliver some dreadful news.

Before they even reached the boarding house, Jacob could hear coughing from within. He exchanged glances with Dr. Harvey, the older man furrowing his brows together before pushing open the front door. The inside of the main part of the boarding house was very dimly lit. The two windows in the room had been covered with the shutters, the few candles around the room the only source of light.

The boarding house was first a log cabin that had been built onto over the years. It had an upstairs with four bedrooms, and there were three downstairs as well. Mr. Cricket rented the rooms out to men who worked up in the mountains, and these men often shared the rooms, sometimes there were four men per room. That was a lot of people in a small amount of space, Jacob thought as he walked in and approached Mr. Cricket as he sat down at a writing desk on the far side of the room.

"How's it going, Mr. Cricket?" Dr. Harvey asked as he approached the man.

The boarding house owner looked over his shoulder as Jacob and Dr. Harvey approached. He then began to cough into the handkerchief he held in one hand as he tried to write with the other.

"I've been better, Doc," Mr. Cricket said in a gravelly voice. Jacob kept his distance as Dr. Harvey approached the man and peered down at him.

"Seems like a few of your boarders have come down with some sort of cough," Dr. Harvey said as he examined Mr. Cricket closely. The man often had greasy hair that he kept combed to the side. But today it seemed that he hadn't paid much attention to his personal hygiene. His muslin shirt was untucked from his trousers, and his suspenders hung loosely on his shoulders. It seemed like Mr. Cricket certainly had seen better days.

"Everyone's been coughing these last few days, and it's only been getting worse," Mr. Cricket said right before he went into a coughing fit. When Dr. Harvey tried patting his back to knock loose whatever might be in his lungs, Mr. Cricket simply swatted him away. "I just thought some of the miners were dealing with the dust of the mountain, but it seems everyone has it now." The man weaved as he talked and then began to write furiously on the paper once more.

"When did this all begin, Mr. Cricket?" Dr. Harvey asked.

"I had a few women sent down to the boarding house to entertain some of the boarders," Mr. Cricket began to explain as he wrote. "One of them seemed sick but performed her duties, nonetheless. Seems like my associate down south double-crossed me and sent me a sickly one to disturb my business." Jacob could hardly believe what he was hearing. He had no idea that Mr. Cricket was paying for prostitutes for his boarders. Dr. Harvey gave Jacob a fierce look, as though to warn him from making a move with his stern eyes.

"When did you say these women came into town?" Dr. Harvey asked.

"The first one came three, no four days ago. The second day before yesterday. Both rode in on the afternoon stagecoach," Mr. Cricket said as he finished writing his letter. He began to seal it as another coughing fit rattled through his body. When it was over, he said, "Now if you'll excuse me, I have a letter to post."

"Let me take care of that for you," Dr. Harvey said as he plucked it out of the man's hands. "Last thing we need is more people getting sick. I'll need you to come with me to the clinic along with any other men that might have the same symptoms as you."

"I have no time for games," Mr. Cricket said right before he started to cough once more. This time though, the man couldn't seem to catch his breath and went tumbling to the ground. Jacob did his best to reach out to the man before he could fall, but with only one arm, he couldn't manage to hold him. The moment Mr. Cricket hit the floor, he lost consciousness. Dr. Harvey knelt by his side, trying to roll him onto his back. But by the time Dr. Harvey had managed it, it was clear that Mr. Cricket was already gone.

"Jesus," Jacob hissed as he took a step back. "He was breathing just a second ago."

"His heart must have given out and couldn't take all the coughing he was doing," Dr. Harvey said as he forced the man's eyelids closed. "I'll get Curtis Denver to help me carry the body over to the clinic."

"I'll go over there for you," Jacob offered. "Should we search the boarding house for any others."

"Probably isn't a bad idea. I'll look into the rooms and you go grab Curtis for me."

"Sure thing, Doc." Jacob took several steps back, his eyes glancing around the room as though to spot other dead bodies. He didn't like the idea of something like a cough being able to kill people.

Jacob left the boarding house in a hurry, his worst fears running through his mind. Jacob wondered who could be next and how many people had been affected by this sickness. He'd hate for anyone else to lose their life, and though Mr. Cricket wasn't the most ideal citizen, Jacob didn't think the man deserved to die like this.

Jacob was relieved when he stepped into the butcher's shop to see that it was currently empty. The small building had white-washed walls, and a fresh vase of flowers sat on the serving counter, their fragrance of lavender and honeysuckle filling the air. Curtis always kept a very clean space, and the shop always looked and smelled inviting.

Jacob could hear the sound of a hatchet coming down hard on a table and thought that Curtis must be in the back of the shop butchering some animal. He didn't want to scare the man, so he rang the bell on the counter.

The soft sound filled the air and summoned Curtis from his work. Washing his hands and arms in a fresh pail of water, he made himself presentable before moving to the front of the shop.

"Hello there, Sheriff," Curtis said once he saw who had come into his shop. "Come for those pork chops you're always so fond of?" Jacob gave him a weak smile.

"Wish that was the case, Curtis," Jacob replied. "Dr. Harvey is over at the boarding house. Mr. Cricket has just passed away and the Doc needs your help getting the man back over to the clinic." Curtis' brows furrowed together at the news. "No! What did he die of? He came into the shop just yesterday to purchase beef steaks, and all he seemed to have was a cough. Well, let me get things cleaned up here and I can head over right away." Curtis reached below his serving counter and pulled out a small sign that read, "I'll Be Right Back." He placed it on the counter before tugging off his apron. Curtis was a tower of a man, tall with broad shoulders. The apron appeared small on him and Jacob wondered if the man had problems with finding clothes that would fit his tall stature.

"Thank you, Curtis. I have to go and let the Mayor know of the death." Jacob tipped his Stetson to Curtis before leaving the butcher shop. Curtis nodded in return, fearing a sense of dread of what he was about to discover when he went over to the boarding house.

Jacob was in a hurry as he walked across town. He saw Tanner coming out of the town hall just as he was coming up to it. The Mayor was stepping out with him, making Jacob curious about where the two of them were headed next.

"Just the man I wanted to see, Sheriff," Mr. Demetri Franklin said as Jacob reached them. "Tanner didn't have the greatest news for me."

"And I certainly won't have much better," Jacob said, feeling a grim pressure applying to his shoulder, a hard expression settling onto his face.

"I went over to the boarding house with Dr. Harvey and watched Mr. Cricket die before me," said Jacob. "He was in a coughing fit and died when it seemed he couldn't breathe anymore." Tanner and Demetri gasped at the news. They were both clearly shocked, and just the thought of watching the man pass away was still a disturbing thought in Jacob's mind.

"Before the man keeled over, he told us that he'd purchased two women from someone down south. The women had come into town on the stagecoach, one two days before the other and both entertained the men at the boarding house. Mr. Cricket said that both of them had been coughing but that no one paid that detail much attention. Now, most of the men at the boarding house are in the clinic with the cough, and Mr. Cricket is dead. I asked Curtis to help Dr. Harvey carry the body over to the clinic."

"What a disaster," Demetri declared. "How could a cough kill someone?"

"I guess if you can't catch your breath, it's like suffocating," Tanner spoke up in a soft voice. Jacob eyed him, thinking that Tanner was losing his nerve with the gruesome details.

"The way I see it, there is just a bunch of sick men right now because of what they decided to indulge in. Might the Good Lord be punishing those who have sinned this way?" Demetri said. Jacob wasn't one to judge, but he wasn't as religious as the Mayor was.

"I think the people need to know to stay away from the clinic for a while," Jacob said then. "I don't want to scare anyone, but no one should be going anywhere near the place if it's not an emergency." Demetri nodded and started to rub his chin.

"I'll go make up a sign with some writing paper and post it on the clinic door," Tanner volunteered.

"Good man, Tanner. I plan to be about simply to answer any questions if need be. I want to reassure everyone that people are just sick and nothing more," Jacob decided.

"Do you think the Marshall should be notified?" Demetri asked.

Jacob shook his head, thinking that it wasn't necessary at the moment. "As long as those that are sick stay away from others that are healthy, it's just a matter of letting people rest and recover."

"Well, as long as no one else dies," Demetri replied. "Keep me updated." The Mayor nodded to both gentlemen before turning around and making his way back to the town hall. He wanted to start writing up a plan of action if this sickness did happen to get out of control.

"I'm going to post myself outside the clinic. Head over to the Sheriff's Office and get that writing paper you need," Jacob said as he turned towards Tanner. "I will probably need to be available in case Dr. Harvey needs an extra hand." Tanner simply nodded before he made his way to the Sheriff's Office. Jacob watched him go, seeing the stiffness in the deputy's shoulders. He wasn't sure what was troubling his deputy, but he hoped that he'd be able to continue to rely on him if this situation did turn into a crisis.

As Jacob made his way over to the clinic and leaned up against the hitching post, he could hear the men inside coughing away. The sound was eerie to listen to since it was the same sound that Mr. Cricket had made right before he died. He watched people moving up and down the boardwalk on the other side of the road. He tried to keep his composure and look friendly as people eyed him. Keeping up pleasant appearances would be key to making sure no one spread any false rumors.

As Jacob rested upon the hitching post, he hoped that Rosa was starting to feel better. He thought about their time together the previous day, thinking that it was nice to spend part of his day with a pretty young lady. He wasn't sure what was going to happen with everyone that was sick, but he still wanted to spend at least part of his days getting to know Rosa better and seeing if they could have a future together. He'd check in with her at the Inn later. Perhaps they could dine together after the customers had been attended to..

When the clinic door opened behind him, Jacob turned to see Dr. Harvey walking out through the clinic. He looked tired and exhausted, and Jacob was eager to hear what the medical man was thinking. Tanner was just coming back over from the Sheriff's Office, a large sheet of writing paper in his hands. He didn't say anything as he handed it to Dr. Harvey. He examined it right before nodding and handing it back to the young man. Tanner didn't hesitate before poking a hole through the paper as he hung it on the nail that stuck out from the door where the doctor would often hang his 'out of the office' sign. Even from where Jacob rested on the hitching post, he could read the large words on the piece of paper.

Clinic closed until further notice. Please direct all emergencies to the Sheriff's Office.

As Jacob read it, he hoped that things weren't going to become too busy at the clinic. He silently prayed that everyone in Bear Creek would be doing their best to stay safe and out of harm's way in order to not overload the doctor while he worked with those who were already sick.

"Curtis helped me carry in Mr. Cricket from the boarding house through the back door of the clinic. He can be buried this evening. Just wish the pastor was in town to give the man his final rights," Dr. Harvey said. "I'm going to try my best to keep the men inside and settled."

"I'll remain outside in case anyone else tries to get into the clinic," Jacob offered.

"I appreciate that, Sheriff." Dr. Harvey looked so weary that Jacob wasn't certain the older man could go on like this. He wondered if he should really telegram the Marshall to see about getting an extra doctor to come spend some time in Bear Creek.

"Tanner, ride up to the mine and let Edward James know about the situation. I bet he's wondering why a good portion of his workers didn't make it there today. He should know to send anyone else who might be sick to the clinic to rest till everyone can get over this cough. But please impress on him how important his discretion in the matter will be," Jacob said

Tanner was relieved to hear this since he felt an itch to get out of town. A deadly sickness had taken both of his parents and the sound of anyone coughing hard always made him remember the night he lost them.

"I'll be back in a bit then," Tanner said as he nodded to both men. Then he quickly made his way towards the livery stables.

"Well, I best get back in there. Holler if you need anything," Dr. Harvey said with a sigh. Jacob watched as the older man turned then and headed back inside the clinic. As he opened the door, the barking sound of coughing men became louder for the short moment the door was opened. Jacob winced, starting to dislike the sound more and more. As he turned his attention back on the town, he only hoped that things would only get better from here.

CHAPTER 10

*B*y the time Rosa awoke the next morning, she was starting to feel more like herself. She sniffled as she sat up and stifled a cough, thinking that she'd become a bit stuffy from sleeping for so long. She washed and dressed in her day gown.

As Rosa fixed up her hair, braiding her long curls, she reasoned that she better show Mrs. Tibet that she was a fine assistant since she'd needed to collapse the previous evening. The last thing she wanted her employer to think was that she was incapable of working in a demanding kitchen. Though Rosa didn't think working at the inn was very strenuous, she nonetheless wanted to make a good impression anytime she could.

After Rosa had finished dressing and looked presentable, she put on her apron and left the bedroom. She could hear idle chatter coming from the dining room, and as she stopped by the door of the kitchen and turned her brown eyes towards the large room, she could see that there were a few patrons for breakfast. Thinking this was a good thing, Rosa made her way into the kitchen to see how she could help Mrs. Tibet.

"Hello, dear. Are you feeling better?" Mrs. Tibet asked the moment she walked through the double doors. Rosa nodded to reassure the older woman, doing her best to keep her chuckle to herself.

"I'm quite better, thank you," Rosa replied. "It only seemed that I was still exhausted from my travels." "That's very understandable," Mrs. Tibet said then proceeded to tell Rosa the menu for that evening and what it was going to be necessary to prepare. "Roast, veggies, and fresh bread is what's on the menu for tonight. I normally like to serve two options, but I have a feeling it isn't on the cards for today. Did you see how few we had in for breakfast?"

"There may be more than you expect," Rosa said, but she was sure Mrs. Tibet was experienced in working out how many diners she would be cooking for. She started to prepare vegetables, wondering if Jacob would be calling in.

"Don't worry about slicing them too big, dear. I often like to serve a healthy serving." Rosa nodded as she did the work, wanting to do as her employer said. She was thinking that Mrs. Tibet was a very generous woman, very different from Mrs. Trevino, who would instruct the kitchen staff to serve small portions.

Soon, Rosa became lost in the rhythm of preparing, cooking and serving the food that Mr. Tibet would come into the kitchen for. Since there was only one menu that evening, it was simple enough work. With two women in the kitchen, Rosa was able to prepare each plate while Mrs. Tibet sliced the roast and divided out the veggies. At one point, Mrs. Tibet also made sure there was enough for herself, Mr. Tibet, and Rosa. She hadn't spoken to Mrs. Tibet about pay and hoped that not too much would be docked for enjoying a meal with her employer as well. Until she found a place of her own with a decent kitchen, she'd have to rely on the food at the inn as well.

"Miss Casey. It seems you have a visitor," Mr. Tibet said at one point in the evening. Rosa had just finished eating between serving plates of food and set her dirty dish in the dry sink when Mr. Tibet had come to tell her the good news. Rosa turned towards him, a genuine smile on her face as she thought that Jacob must have come by the inn to see her. All day she had been wondering if he would call and felt disappointed that he didn't. Then told herself not to expect a busy Sheriff to spare the time to pay her a visit.

"Thank you, Mr. Tibet," Rosa said as she walked out of the kitchen, making sure to wipe her hands on her apron so she looked presentable enough. In the foyer, she found Jacob standing near the inn door. He smiled at her as she came towards him but Rosa could see that Jacob was exhausted and felt surprised that he'd paid her a visit at all.

"Good evening, Rosa," Jacob said as she approached. A part of him had wanted to wait till tomorrow to visit with her again, but after everything that had happened today, he really wanted to end the day on a good note.

"Hello, Jacob," Rosa replied. "Pardon me for being so forward, but you look exhausted." Jacob chuckled as he nodded.

"It's been one heck of a day," he admitted. "Care to sit with me while I enjoy something to eat?"

"I'd be happy to," Rosa replied. She walked with Jacob into the dining room. Most of the patrons had gone for the evening, leaving the large room to just the two of them. Mr. Tibet came over and informed Jacob of the meal for the day. He said he would settle for that.

"Planning on being up all night?" Rosa asked when Jacob ordered a small cup of coffee with his meal.

"I want to be ready for anything if it does happen," Jacob answered. "There's been all sorts of things going on today that I feel like I need to be ready for anything."

"Like what?" Rosa asked. She was curious about what could possibly happen in such a small town as Bear Creek. Her mind started to race as she tried to think of something before Jacob had a chance to answer her.

For a few minutes Jacob simply watched Rosa, trying to decide how honest he should be with her. If they truly were going to have a serious relationship, he should be willing to be completely honest with her. However, he didn't want to scare her right at the start of her stay in Bear Creek.

"Well, to be honest, I'm not quite entirely sure. I'd received a telegram from the Marshall of the territory, warning me about bank robbers before I met you yesterday morning," Jacob explained. Rosa placed her hand over her mouth, thinking that was terrible news.

"Is the Marshall worried about them coming to Bear Creek?"

"I think the Marshall was just letting all the sheriffs know. That's what he does when he gets wind of any kind of trouble."

"Well, at least he is thoughtful enough to let others know," Rosa reasoned.

"He sure is a great Marshall. And we're lucky to have a telegram machine here in Bear Creek." Jacob realized his error the moment he spoke. He was already thinking of Rosa as one of the town's people. Rosa picked up on that and thought it was nice to be included with the others in the area. After all, she had no intentions of returning to Boston.

Mr. Tibet came then and gave Jacob his cup of coffee. He enjoyed the boost it gave him then told Rosa the situation that had arisen with the sick miners. She listened carefully, trying to tell herself that she felt perfectly well. But she really didn't. "There weren't nearly as many men taking breakfast today," she said.

"The doctor is looking after those that are ill at the clinic."

"I think they are all staying over at the clinic till they feel better. I had the opportunity to speak with Dr. Harvey a few times. He's given them something to help them sleep," Jacob explained. He didn't want to tell Rosa about the fact that Mr. Cricket had died or the fact he'd hired women to entertain men at the boarding house.

"Well, I hope they are feeling better soon," said Rosa. "There's nothing worse than getting sick in the springtime when it's finally warm enough to enjoy the outdoors."

"I'd agree to that," Jacob said right as Mr. Tibet returned with his plate of food. "But that's enough about my day. How was yours? Everything working out for you with Mrs. Tibet?"

"Working with Mrs. Tibet is easy enough. It's more of learning how she prefers things. She's teaching me a lot about cooking for a large group of people and working with the ingredients that are readily available." Jacob listened as he ate, not wanting Rosa to think that he was insensitive.

"I've never been to a big city like Boston before, but I hear that there are markets where people just buy what they need every day instead of keeping a garden or making good relationships with the farmers in the area."

"That would be correct," Rosa confirmed. "Cook would have one of the footmen go out each morning to collect the things that weren't already grown in the garden. Mrs. Trevino kept a marvelous garden with many flowers." Jacob chuckled at the thought, thinking that the only flowers that were kept in Bear Creek were the ones that grew wild in the open plains.

"I know that things are not the same here as they are in Boston, but I hope you'll come to enjoy it here nonetheless." Rosa looked at Jacob then, really looking at the way he smiled at her. She wasn't sure just yet what to make of him, but he had a way of making her feel at ease.

"I think I will," Rosa commented as she looked away from him. "The work is easy enough."

"Have you talked to Mr. and Mrs. Tibet yet about payment?"

"Not yet. I have enough that I brought with me that I should be comfortable for a while. But payment is a part of what I'd like to discuss with the couple this evening."

"Good. With the mine up and running, and the inn completely full once more, I'm sure they'd be able to afford a good pay for you."

"Either way, it's simply nice to keep busy," Rosa admitted. "I'm so used to having a full day of chores that I'm not sure what to do with myself during the day now that I'm not responsible for someone other than myself." Jacob smiled, an idea coming to mind as he listened to Rosa.

"Well, if you're not too busy tomorrow, how about you join me for an evening walk? There is a small hill north of town that we can walk to from town. It's a great spot to watch the sun set." Rosa couldn't contain her smile as she thought about the idea. It was probably the most romantic thing anyone had ever asked her to do and she couldn't help but nod.

"I'd be delighted," she replied with. "I'll tell Mrs. Tibet about it this evening so that she could see if she could do without me for a small bit."

"I'm sure that Mrs. Tibet would be happy to oblige once you tell her whom you're meeting. If not, you can tell her it's official Sheriff's business that you can't refuse." Rosa laughed openly then, and Jacob thought it was the most beautiful sound in the world.

"My goodness. You seem to be a troublemaker, mixing business with pleasure," Rosa said. She felt daring and wanted to see how Jacob would respond to her flirting. He raised an eyebrow at her, surprised that she had become so forward with her words. But he liked that Rosa was becoming comfortable enough with him to be a bit playful.

"I might be a sheriff, but I like to think I can still surprise people with my ability to be a little bit of a troublemaker," he replied.

"I hope you're not willing to prove yourself to just anyone." Rosa leaned forward as she placed her elbows on the table and cradled her chin in her hands. She flashed her eyelashes at him, making a lopsided smile appear on Jacob's face.

"No, not just anyone," Jacob confirmed in a soft voice, becoming mesmerized by Rosa's beauty. The worries of the day just seemed to fade away while he was with Rosa. He wished he could stay like this forever, simply spending time with the person who had completely captured his interest.

"Well, that is a relief to hear." Rosa stood from the table then as she took Jacob's empty plate. "I better help out with the dishes and take the time to talk to Mrs. Tibet about my pay. But I'll let her know that we have a date tomorrow evening that I simply cannot miss." Jacob stood with Rosa, thinking that it would be perfect if it was already tomorrow afternoon.

"I look forward to it," is what Jacob settled on saying. He then came close to Rosa, causing her eyes to grow wide as he did so. Then slowly, being mindful of his right arm in the sling, he leaned down and placed a kiss on Rosa's cheek. Rosa was surprised by the kiss. She enjoyed the contact, feeling the warmth of Jacob's body so close to hers and the way his lips lightly touched her cheek. She'd never been kissed before and thought it was quite pleasant.

The sound of someone clearing their throat filled the room. They both quickly turned and Jacob straightened his posture as they saw Mr. Tibet coming into the room. He gave Jacob a stern look, like a father would give a young man who'd just kissed his daughter without first asking for permission. Rosa couldn't help but giggle like a young schoolgirl as she turned her eyes away from Mr. Tibet.

"Have a good evening, Rosa," Jacob said, drawing her attention back to him.

"Good evening," she replied. She then watched as Jacob exchanged a handshake with Mr. Tibet before walking from the room. The older man's eyes softened as he left and turned back to Rosa.

"I'm not afraid to put the fear of God into anyone if the good Sheriff is being too forward," Mr. Tibet admitted.

"Fear not, Mr. Tibet. Jacob has been a perfect gentleman," Rosa reassured him as she made her way into the kitchen to help with the dishes. Mr. Tibet followed after her, passing through the kitchen and heading out back to gather a pail of water to help with cleaning the dishes. A part of him was pleased to see that the Sheriff was being romantic with Rosa since all women deserved to be romanced and courted properly. But he also knew that Rosa was an orphan and had no father of her own to look out for her wellbeing. She might have just arrived in Bear Creek, but Mr. Tibet was the type of man who was always willing to stand up for a woman's virtue.

"How's the Sheriff this evening?" Mrs. Tibet asked when Rosa joined her at the dry sink. Mrs. Tibet plunged her hands in the warm soapy water and scrubbed at the dishes. She then handed the clean ones to Rosa to dry and put away.

"Jacob is doing well," Rosa replied. "He's asked me to accompany him to see the sunset tomorrow."

"Oh, how romantic," Mrs. Tibet said in a cheery voice. "Mr. Tibet and I might be well into our later years, but you'd be surprised how romantic the man can still be." The women chuckled together as Mr. Tibet came in then, carrying a fresh pail of water.

"Sounds like mischief to me," Mr. Tibet said as they both looked at him. Mr. Tibet winked at his wife as he set the pail of water on the counter for her. Rosa hadn't really paid much attention to the interaction of married couples because Mr. and Mrs. Trevino were always so busy. But now she could see the loving interaction between Mr. and Mrs. Tibet.

"We're just talking about Miss Casey being invited by the Sheriff to watch the sunset tomorrow," Mrs. Tibet explained.

"Well isn't that something," Mr. Tibet said as he placed his hands on his hips. "I didn't think Jacob could be a softy like that, but I guess the good sheriff can still surprise me." Rosa took another dish from Mrs. Tibet and proceeded to dry it, her eyes turned down as she did her best not to blush. It felt nice to be the recipient of someone's affections and to see that action respected by others in the community.

Rosa turned her head quickly away from the dishes she was drying as she sneezed. She quickly put away the dish she was holding and reached into her pocket for her handkerchief and blew her nose. Then she drew her hand across her forehead, it had started to ache and once again she felt as though she might be suffering from a fever, the way she had the previous day. Maybe it wasn't still the exhaustion from her journey to Montana.

"Are you okay, my dear?" Mrs. Tibet asked as she handed Rosa another plate to dry.

"Oh yes," Rosa reassured her. "A change of scenery can often cause someone to sneeze for a bit."

"When I was a boy, my older brother could never help us harvest the hay in the fall. He'd get all stuffy and sneezy, becoming completely incapable of being anywhere around fresh cut hay," Mr. Tibet spoke up. "I reckon that being in a new place can cause the same things to happen."

"That is my thought as well," Rosa said, glad that the two of them were such understanding people. Mrs. Trevino did not care all that much if one of her servants became sick. She still always expected the same performance out of anyone unless they were deathly ill.

"Well, you enjoy your time tomorrow with Jacob," Mrs. Tibet said. "It's not every day you get invited by a charming man to watch the sunset."

"That is true," Rosa agreed as she pocketed her handkerchief and began to help dry the dishes once more. "But since I have you both together, I wanted to ask you what you thought would be the pay for helping in the kitchen?" Rosa watched as Mr. and Mrs. Tibet exchanged a look as though they were communicating silently with one another.

"Business has been good ever since the mine opened back up," Mr. Tibet said as he focused on Rosa. "The rooms upstairs are always booked, and many people come to dine as well. And I can see that things go easier with two women in the kitchen." Mrs. Tibet nodded, agreeing fully with her husband. She knew she wasn't a spring chicken anymore and Rosa's help had been greatly appreciated.

"Therefore, we've talked about offering you two dollars a week in return for helping Mrs. Tibet every day. We won't charge you for staying at the inn or taking meals with us because we understand you're here to court with Jacob and won't be staying at the inn forever," Mr. Tibet finished. Rosa thought about the terms and thought that the older couple was being very generous. Not only would they not charge her for room and board, but they were willing to pay her a small amount on top of that.

"I think that is a very lovely offer," Rosa agreed. "I'm not sure how long it will be before Jacob and I know if things will work out between us, but I promise to be an ardent worker every day." Mrs. and Mr. Tibet both gave Rosa a pleased smile. Mrs. Tibet liked to see how eager Rosa was and thought she would make a good wife for Jacob.

Once the kitchen was cleaned up and ready for the next day's work, Rosa bid the older couple goodnight and made her way to her bedroom. She was feeling good about how the day had gone and thought she could finally relax with the knowledge that things were turning out good for her in Bear Creek. It had only been the first of days, but Rosa could easily see herself helping Mrs. Tibet each day in the kitchen and using her spare time to visit with Jacob. He was not only a handsome man, but he had a good sense of humor, too. And the way he was well respected in town went a long way with Rosa to help her feel that Jacob was truly a good man.

After readying for bed, Rosa slid underneath the covers right as she sneezed once more and then fell to a fit of coughing. She lay in bed with pain throbbing in her head and hating the thought that she might be coming down with any sort of sickness. It couldn't be more inconvenient to come down with anything. She'd traveled so far without any issues when it came to sickness that Rosa hoped dearly that her sneezing only had to do with coming to live in a new place. She was so eager to see Jacob tomorrow and to enjoy the sunset together that it took some time for Rosa to finally fall asleep.

CHAPTER 11

*J*acob had barely set the kettle on the stove in the Sheriff's Office when someone began to knock on the door. Jacob called over his shoulder, telling the person to enter so he could finish making his morning cup of coffee. He'd been up all night worrying about the town that he'd hardly gotten any sleep. It also didn't help that he couldn't get comfortable enough for a really good night's sleep.

"Morning, Sheriff," came the voice of Edward James as he stepped into the office. Jacob turned as the man shut the door behind him. For a man who worked in the mines every day, Edward always dressed nicely when he was in town. He and his sister had a small cabin up in the mountains and rarely came to town. It was also no secret that Edward was part Indian, encouraging him to spend more time with his workers and the local Sioux tribe.

"Morning, Edward. What brings you in this early?" Jacob asked as he finished making the pot of coffee. Now he just needed to wait for the grounds to give up their flavor to the boiling water.

"I got word from Tanner about some of my men being sick. Thought I'd stop into town this morning to see how they are doing, but I noticed the sign on the clinic door. Figured I'd come by here to get the full story." Jacob nodded, thinking that was quite logical.

"I haven't been over this morning to see how things are, but yesterday all the miners in the boarding house went over to the clinic to get checked out by Dr. Harvey for their cough. Unfortunately, the cough really got to Mr. Cricket and he passed away." Edward looked very concerned at hearing this. "That's dreadful. I've never been particularly fond of the man but that boarding house is a mighty convenient place for my miners to stay. Is the cough that deadly?" Edward then asked as he folded his arms over his chest.

"I can't say that for sure, Edward," Jacob honestly replied. "No one else has died from the cough. It might just be a temporary illness and those affected will have to take time to rest and recover." Jacob looked at the worried man. "I can appreciate your worries. If the men aren't able to work the mines, then your progress will be greatly cut back, just when everything was going so well."

"You've said it! Care to join me on checking in on them?" Edward asked. Jacob would have preferred to enjoy his morning cup of coffee before starting any official business, but he too was curious to see how the sick miners were faring.

After putting on his Stetson, Jacob followed Edward out of the office. As they passed through town, Jacob waved to those that were already up and active that morning. Mr. Fry was putting his open sign on the front porch while Mr. Tibet crossed the main street on his way to the butcher. Jacob needed to keep up appearances, especially since he was walking with a man that didn't often come to town as they headed towards the clinic.

As they approached the front door, Jacob could hear the familiar sound of coughing coming from within. He'd hoped that the worst of it would have been over by now, but as the sound continued, Jacob had little hope that the miners were much better today. Edward knocked loudly on the door as they came onto the front porch. A second later, the door was cracked open just enough for the men to get a clear view of Dr. Harvey.

"Is this an emergency?"

Jacob thought the man sounded panicked and he looked exhausted. In fact he didn't look as though he would be very useful to anyone who was in dire need.

"No, Dr. Harvey. I've just come to see how my workers are," Edward explained.

"Not much better, I'm afraid," Dr. Harvey admitted. "Two men passed away in the night because of it." Jacob's mouth fell open as the news settled over him. *Two more had died from a cough?* Jacob could hardly believe what he was hearing. "It's best if people stay away until it either claims them all or it finally passes."

"What is being done to treat them?" Edward asked as his brows furrowed together.

"They've all been given laudanum to help with the pain and to keep them relaxed or sleeping,"

"I don't like the sound of that," said Edward. "Surely if they're coughing, they need to be awake to cough up whatever is in their bodies that's causing the problem?" He turned to the Sheriff. "No wonder that people are dying."

The doctor leant against the door frame and drew a handkerchief over his sweating face.

"Would you be willing to try a different method, Doctor?" Edward asked. "I might have an idea.".

"I'm willing to hear what you might have to say, Edward, but don't hold it against me when I don't take the advice of someone who isn't a doctor," Dr. Harvey replied as he narrowed his eyes at the young man.

"When I was a child, I got a really bad cough from playing outside in the rain. My mother converted our teepee into a hot space with many pots of boiling water to fill it with steam. In the pots were several different kinds of mint leaves to help me breathe easier and to help me cough out the yuck that was in my body. Let me talk to Brown Bear about bringing a teepee down to the clinic to try the same thing."

Jacob remembered that Edward's mother had been a Sioux Indian, which was one of the reasons he had been able to open up the mine after the terrible confrontation between the previous miners and the

Indians. He saw the doctor try to grapple with the idea that had been proposed. "These sick miners are real weary and that might put too much stress on their bodies." Then he straightened up. "But at this point, it wouldn't hurt to try, either. So, yes, I say give it a go," Dr. Harvey agreed. "I really don't want to see anyone else die because of this cough."

Edward shook the man's hand. "I'm relieved, doctor. Traditional Indian remedies can often assist Western medicines.

"I will ride straight to the Indian camp and speak with Brown Bear. I'm sure he will be willing to help," Edward said. He then nodded to both men before stepping off the porch and hurrying towards his horse. Jacob turned his attention back on the doctor, seeing his age clearly reflected on his face.

"Doesn't sound like any other cough I've heard about before," Jacob said, wanting to know what the doctor really thought about the situation.

"I'm not quite sure myself, Sheriff," Dr. Harvey admitted. "It's not the time of year for coughing, and even a good night's rest doesn't seem to help." He pushed his few strands of hair across his pate. "I fear for the infection spreading and causing more deaths." Dr. Harvey suddenly placed his mouth into the crook of his elbow and gave a barking cough, startling Jacob.

"Oh, Doc. Don't tell me you have it, too," Jacob said as he stepped forward to open the clinic door and see what he could do to help the doctor. But the older man waved him off as his coughing subsided.

"It's part of the job, Jacob," Dr. Harvey said sternly. "It's not the first time I've gotten the same sickness as my patients. You just keep people away from the clinic and all should be well. Now go. It's one thing for the town to lose a doctor, another if it lost a sheriff as well." He shut the door in Jacob's shocked face.

Jacob stood on the porch of the clinic, simply staring at the closed door as he listened to the sound of the men coughing within. He couldn't quite believe that this was happening, that two more miners had died from the cough and that Dr. Harvey had it as well. His eyes focused on the note Tanner had posted on the door, thinking that a better version was needed for anyone coming anywhere near the clinic.

Jacob finally made his way back over to the Sheriff's Office. When he stepped inside, he found Tanner pouring himself a cup of coffee. He looked at the younger man and thought how he'd hate to lose any of the people he'd grown close to over the years. This town wouldn't survive if the most important people passed away.

"Looks like you've had a rough morning," Tanner spoke up as Jacob shut the door and settled into his chair behind his desk. Tanner poured him a cup of coffee and set it before him. Jacob picked up the tin carefully with his left hand and took a few sips as he thought about how he was going to explain this all to Tanner.

"Edward James paid me a visit this morning. I went over with him to the clinic to check on how the miners had faired overnight," Jacob started with. "Dr. Harvey opened the clinic door just wide enough to explain that two more miners had died, and that people need to stay clear of the clinic. Seems the doc also has the cough now."

Tanner stared at Jacob with wide eyes. "This has to be some sort of nightmare," he said.

"Edward has gone up to talk to Brown Bear about bringing a teepee down to turn into some sort of sweat hut. He explained that it helped him as a child with his bad cough and might help the miners."

Tanner swallowed the rest of his coffee and set the cup aside before settling down at his desk.

"What do you think we should do in the meantime?" Tanner asked.

Jacob thought hard about this question, trying to think of what the best option would be.

"First, we need to keep people away from the clinic so no one else catches the sickness," Jacob determined. "I want to telegram the Marshall and let him know of the situation in case he knows of any doctors that could come to town and aid Dr. Harvey. The Mayor should be notified as well."

"So, which one of us is going to be posted outside the clinic?" Tanner asked in a shaky voice.

"Since I can't really ride a horse right now, or write a letter, I'll leave you to run all the errands," Jacob said, noticing the way Tanner had paled at the idea of having to stand guard outside the clinic. He was determined to understand his deputy's fear but figured that right now wasn't the time. Tanner let out a sigh of relief to know that he could be the one to get all the work done while Jacob made sure no one came near the clinic.

"Well, I best get to it," Tanner said as he stood and made his way to the door. "I could even try to meet up with Edward to see if the Indians need any help carrying things to town."

"I'm sure any assistance would be appreciated," Jacob reasoned. Tanner simply nodded once before hurrying out of the Sheriff's Office. Jacob took the time to enjoy his coffee, knowing that this would probably be the only time in the day where he'd be able to sit and just be still for a moment. He wasn't sure what else would happen today, but he hoped that after everything he'd still get to take Rosa to go see the sunset right outside of town.

Jacob fixed his Stetson as he stood and put his tin cup back on the stove. He then made his way out of the office, making sure to lock it behind him before heading over to the clinic to keep watch. If anything, he hoped that no one else would end up dead. Especially the town's only doctor.

WHEN ROSA WAS AWAKENED by the morning call of the rooster, she groaned from the pain that had formed in the back of her head. It made her eyes sensitive to the morning light that peered through the curtains of the window. She raised her head off the pillow, feeling how sore and tired her neck and shoulders felt. It was as though she had slept on a pile of rocks instead of a comfortable bed.

Slowly, Rosa got out of bed, not bothering to pull back the curtains. She wasn't looking forward to seeing any light as the little bit that had made its way into her room was already hurting her tired eyes. She took her time getting dressed because everything felt so sore in her body. Rosa's nose was runny, and she had to frequently blow her nose to clear it.

Rosa was on her third handkerchief when someone knocked on her door. She turned towards the bedroom door and tried to call out, to ask the visitor for just one more moment till she could finish getting dressed. But all that came out of her throat was a wet cough that overtook her body. Rosa was so surprised that it took several moments for her to regain her composure long enough to finish dressing and pull open the bedroom door with her mouth covered by a handkerchief.

"Miss Casey, are you feeling alright?" Mrs. Tibet asked as Rosa opened the door all the way. "I became worried when you didn't show for breakfast."

"Forgive me, Mrs. Tibet. I don't know what has come over me," Rosa said just before she turned her head and began to cough hard into her handkerchief. Mrs. Tibet came to her and started to pat her on the back, trying to clear anything that might have gotten stuck. It was a while before the cough subsided and Rosa could catch her breath again.

"Why don't you lie down and I'll send Mr. Tibet over to fetch Dr. Harvey to take a look at you," Mrs. Tibet offered. Rosa only nodded as she lay back on the bed. Her head was pounding from the pain that seemed to be blooming right behind her eyes. She felt dizzy and wasn't sure what to do with herself. She'd been sick before, but nothing quite like this.

"I'll be back shortly. I'm just going to let Mr. Tibet know and then I'll get you something for breakfast," Mrs. Tibet said in a sorrowful voice. "I hate for anyone to be sick and sure hope, young lady, that you feel alright after a good meal."

Rosa didn't respond as she laid her head down and closed her eyes. She couldn't fathom what was happening to her and hoped she wasn't getting sick like the miners.

JACOB WAS SITTING on the front porch stairs of the clinic when he saw Mr. Tibet hurry out of the inn and make his way quickly in his direction. He didn't like the way Mr. Tibet looked worried as Jacob pushed himself onto his feet. It had been a rather quiet morning after he'd posted himself outside the clinic and hoped that Mr. Tibet wasn't on his way to share bad news with him.

"Is Dr. Harvey in?" Mr. Tibet asked as he approached the clinic. "Mrs. Tibet just sent me over. Seems Miss Casey is very under the weather." Jacob felt like the air had been knocked out of his lungs in one swift motion. Could Rosa be sick, too?

"Dr. Harvey has asked to keep anyone who doesn't have an emergency out of the clinic. There are some very sick miners inside and no one should go in there unless they want to get sick, too," Jacob explained.

"Well, Miss Casey is coughing up a storm. I'm afraid she needs some sort of medicine real bad," Mr. Tibet pleaded. Jacob ran his fingers through his hair, thinking that this was his worst nightmare coming true. How could Rosa have gotten sick like the other miners? She stepped into the clinic yesterday for only a moment. Was that all it took to catch the sickness? Then he remembered the coughing woman who had been in the stagecoach with Rosa. She was as sick as the miners now, and she and the prostitute she'd come to join must have been responsible for bringing the infection to Bear Creek. Fear invaded Jacob's heart. Then he determined that Rosa was not going to die.

"I'll come over with you and check on Rosa myself. There might be a solution that Edward James is working on, but I'm waiting for him to get back into town," Jacob explained. Mr. Tibet didn't seem convinced, but the older man nodded and motioned for Jacob to follow him quickly. Together, they returned to the inn.

As soon as Jacob entered the lobby, he could hear Rosa's barking cough from down the hallway. He shut the inn door and followed after Mr. Tibet until they reached Rosa's room. The bedroom door was open, and Mrs. Tibet was sitting on the edge of the bed, rubbing Rosa's back as she coughed. It sounded as though Rosa was struggling to breathe as she held a handkerchief to her mouth while she coughed. After a moment, she settled once more. Her eyes fluttered open for just a moment, locking with Jacob's before she closed her eyes once more.

"She's been like this all morning," Mrs. Tibet said as she looked up at Jacob from where she sat on the edge of the bed. Her face was wrinkled with concern as she looked up at Jacob.

"How was she yesterday?" Jacob asked as he came over to the bed. Rosa looked pale and clammy, her breath wheezing in and out of her open mouth.

"She was sneezing a bit, and we all just thought she had some sort of allergy from moving to a new town," Mr. Tibet explained.

"And she had a short hot flash earlier in the day. She'd taken a nap and seemed right as rain for the evening meal," Mrs. Tibet added.

Jacob could see the way Rosa struggled to breathe, and when she couldn't seem to take it any longer, she began to cough once more. Her body jerked awake as she held the handkerchief over her mouth and coughed for all she was worth.

"Dr. Harvey has been giving the miners laudanum to help them sleep. Edward James has gone to talk to Brown Bear about another method that might help," Jacob said in a grave voice. He didn't want to tell the older couple that three people had died because of the cough. He was also certain that none of them were safe in the same room with someone this sick.

"I'm afraid that something needs to be done soon to get her some relief," Mrs. Tibet said with tears in her eyes.

"I agree, Mrs. Tibet. I'm going to go now and see what I can do for her. I don't want her to be so sick after traveling so far just to meet me," Jacob admitted in a heavy voice. He felt the weight of the world on his shoulders as this sickness seemed to have spread faster than he could comprehend. And after everything Rosa had been through to reach Bear Creek just three days ago, he wanted to do everything he could for the young woman.

"I'll stay with her and try putting a cold cloth on her head," Mrs. Tibet decided as she moved from the bed and went over to the water basin resting on the dresser. Jacob took one more look at Rosa, pleading silently that she would live through this. When he stepped out of the room, Mr. Tibet followed him to the door.

"Jacob, just how bad is this sickness?" Mr. Tibet asked in a hushed voice. Jacob stopped for a moment and turned towards the older man. Since Rosa was sick and they were taking care of her, Jacob felt that they should only know the truth.

"The miners at the boarding house caught it from a woman who'd come in on the stagecoach," Jacob explained. "They are all sick now with this same cough. Mr. Cricket died the day before yesterday, and Dr. Harvey said this morning that two of the miners had passed away in the night." Mr. Tibet gasped as he covered his mouth with his aged hand. His eyes had grown large, and as they heard Rosa begin to cough again, they both looked towards the bedroom with great fear in their hearts.

"How on earth do you think Miss Casey caught it?" Mr. Tibet wondered out loud.

"She was on the same coach with a woman who had the same cough. She'd come to join a friend, ordered by Mr. Cricket, for the entertainment of his miners. I reckon that's what brought this dreadful sickness to Bear Creek."

"If she shared the coach with someone that sick, I can understand," said Mr. Tibet.

"I don't understand how this sickness works, Mr. Tibet. But I would say for you and Mrs. Tibet to be careful as well," Jacob said as he turned his attention back on the older man. "But I'm going to go find Edward James. He has an idea that might help them all recover."

"I pray to God that he does," Mr. Tibet said very seriously. As they parted ways, Mr. Tibet returned to the bedroom where he watched Mrs. Tibet hold a damp cloth to Rosa's forehead. He wasn't sure what was going to happen next, but he dearly hoped that everyone would be able to recover soon.

CHAPTER 12

*J*acob was trying his best to keep focused on the task at hand instead of worrying about how dreadful Rosa had appeared just moments ago. He left the inn and headed straight for the livery stables. He knew that riding a horse with only one good arm was going to be difficult, but he needed to meet up with Edward and let him know that any help that was coming needed to come to town as soon as possible. God only knew who would become sick next.

"Hey there, Sheriff," came Roger's voice as Jacob made his way into the large barn. He managed the stables and always did a great job at keeping the Sheriff's horse well taken care of.

"Hey, Roger. I need Victor saddled and ready to go. I have important business to take care of," Jacob said as he walked past Roger and went straight to the stall where his horse was being kept. Roger looked startled, for Jacob had not been riding since he'd broken his arm but he obviously understood there was some emergency and had the Sheriff's horse ready to go in just minutes. Roger held the reins for Jacob so the Sheriff could pull himself up into the saddle with his left hand. Once settled, Roger gave him the reins before jogging down to the end of the barn to open the gate.

"Good luck, Sheriff!" Roger called to Jacob as he left the barn at a gallop. Jacob wished he could have at least waved at Roger, but he was more focused on keeping his balance on the horse. He was in a hurry, but he also needed to stay upright in the saddle so he could reach the Indian camp in time to tell Edward and Brown Bear that all the help that could be available was surely needed.

Jacob led his horse up into the mountains. Passing through the tree line, it was like being transported into a whole other world. The density of the trees often made it hard to maneuver through the mountains, but Jacob was familiar with the trails and which ones to take to reach the Indian camp. When he came to the creek that ran straight down from the mountain's top, he looked around, still cautious about running into any other bears. The area looked clear as he led his horse through the creek and onto the other side. The last thing he needed was any more problems or delays.

Jacob didn't bother leaving his horse with the other Indian ponies in the corral as he came into the Indian camp. He pulled his horse to a stop and carefully dismounted. He saw that a group of Indians had gathered around the central fireplace and figured that would be a good place to locate Edward and let him know of Rosa's condition.

As he passed through camp, Jacob was greeted by several of the Indians. After the camp had been attacked by the previous foreman of the mine and his workers, Jacob had become more acquainted with the Indians. He worked with Brown Bear to ensure that his lands stayed protected and that the new miners weren't causing any trouble. Therefore, he'd come to be familiar with many of the Indians, even if he hadn't learned all their names yet.

"Edward," Jacob called out as he neared the central fire. It was here that all the Indians gathered throughout the day to share a meal with one another. It's also where important matters were discussed with the whole tribe and where Jacob found Edward speaking with Brown Bear.

"Has something happened?" Edward asked as he turned to see the Sheriff coming his way.

"Rosa Casey just came in on the same stagecoach three days ago with one of the women that brought the contagion. She's coughing up a storm now, too," Jacob explained. He shifted his eyes to Brown Bear then, the very tall Indian chief with long brown hair and dark eyes that almost appeared black. Brown Bear was an older man, but still very capable of running circles around Jacob.

"I've already told Brown Bear the situation with so many sick and dying. He's agreed to lend us several teepees while the women have started to gather the necessary herbs," Edward explained.

"I'm very sorry to hear about Dr. Harvey becoming sick," Brown Bear said. "He is a good man and is always willing to help anyone regardless of race. White Raven shall accompany you all to town to oversee those who have become sick as well."

"Thank you, Brown Bear," Jacob said. "I fear that Dr. Harvey does not know what else to do."

"And there is much that my people may be able to teach yours," Brown Bear said with a deep grunt, signaling his agreement to this aid. The Indian chief was always looking for ways to impress the white people that lived so close to his people's lands. This could be an opportunity to show that they were a very peaceful people who were willing to help those in need.

"Everyone seems ready to go," Tanner said as he joined them. "What are you doing here, Jacob?"

"Miss Casey also has the cough," Jacob explained. "I came right away to see if I could help with any of the preparations. She needs help badly."

"Fear not, Sheriff," Brown Bear said then. "We shall do everything we can to save those that have become ill." Brown Bear spoke in such a confident way that for a moment Jacob felt a sense of hope that the answer to their problem had been discovered. It had been a very strange and stressful last few days and Jacob wanted to look forward to the end of all this sickness. He especially wanted to make sure that Rosa recovered as quickly as she could. After all she'd been through, she deserved some peace.

"Well fellas, let's be off then," Edward spoke up. Brown Bear spoke in his native tongue to the Indian braves standing close by. Everyone seemed to move into action as supplies were gathered and began to be carried down the mountain. It took Jacob some time to get back into the saddle of his horse with the help of Tanner, but once he was up and ready to go, he followed the parade of Indians that were taking the direct trail to town.

As they all traveled together, it was slow progress going down the mountain since teepees were being carried by hand between several Indian braves. Indian maidens carried wicker baskets of an herb that filled the air with its smell, reminding Jacob of peppermint candies. Other women carried large clay pots while different Indian braves positioned large bundles of logs on their shoulders as though they were preparing to make a large bonfire. It all amazed Jacob how fast the Indians were to move into action and that they were all willing to help the miners when just last year a group of miners had attacked the Indian camp, killing several Indians in the process.

"So, how do you think Miss Casey got sick as well?" Tanner asked as he rode alongside Jacob ready to help if he needed in leading his horse down the mountain with only one good hand. The pace was slow, so Jacob was at least certain he wouldn't have to worry about falling off his horse.

"Rosa came in on the same stagecoach as a woman who was coughing away." Jacob explained about Cricket's hiring of prostitutes for his boarders. "I reckon it was they who brought the infection to Bear Creek and Rosa must have caught it off her fellow traveler. Confined in that small space for that length of time would be a perfect way of catching an infection," Jacob explained.

"It's hard to believe that a sickness could spread so easily and with such quickness," Tanner said as he shook his head. "My parents both went out of town when I was about ten years old to visit with my father's sick parents before they died. When they came back, they were both sick and died shortly afterwards." Jacob had never heard about Tanner's parents before and was surprised by the story. Though, it did explain a lot about the way Tanner had been acting lately.

"I'm truly sorry to hear that," Jacob replied. Though his own parents had passed away only a few years ago, their deaths had been to old age. He didn't like to think what it would have been like to lose them at a young age and feel completely helpless in saving them.

"I had a really good uncle that took me in after they died," Tanner said after a while. "But ever since then I have been very skittish around sick people."

"That's understandable," Jacob reasoned. "But I have confidence in Brown Bear. I'm eager to see how this will work out." Tanner nodded as they continued to make their way through the thick forest and down the mountain to the town.

As they reached the edge of town, they decided the best place to set up the teepees would be behind the clinic. Jacob followed the group of Indians there, guiding and directing the best he could to keep the town's people out of the way and to show everyone where to go.

"What's going on, Sheriff?" Mr. Fry asked as he came out of his shop, his eyes wide at the number of Indians that were passing through and heading to the backyard of the clinic.

"Brown Bear and his people have come to help those that have recently become sick with a terrible cough," Jacob explained. "They're awfully sick, and even Dr. Harvey has come down with the likes of it." Mr. Fry covered his mouth then as he looked at all the Indians passing through town, carrying all manner of things.

"But how could they possibly help?" Mr. Fry asked

"That's why I'm out here to see and keep an eye on things, Mr. Fry. Don't you worry one bit," Jacob tried to reassure the older gentleman. He knew that not everyone in town particularly cared for Indians, and the last thing he wanted was anyone getting angry over what was trying to be done to save people's lives.

"I hope you keep two eyes on them," Mr. Fry said in a stern voice before he turned and quickly headed inside his shop. Jacob sighed, knowing that he couldn't really deal with that problem right now. It wouldn't be a secret for much longer that there were several people who were sick, and eventually the town's people would learn that a few had even died. But if he could do anything to prevent the sickness from spreading or taking any more lives, he was willing to give it a try.

Jacob made his way behind the clinic with the others and sat upon his horse as he watched three teepees be raised on their poles. They were quickly put up by the experienced Indians, and as Jacob watched, he figured that if he had tried to help, he'd only have gotten in the way. Once the teepees were up, the women quickly went to work gathering all the wood that had been brought down from the mountain and then began to create large fires inside each.

"Come, Jacob. See what the women are able to create inside the teepees," Brown Bear said as he walked over to Jacob. Brown Bear was kind enough to hold the horse's reins as Jacob carefully dismounted. He then followed Brown Bear over to one of the teepees and ducked inside after the Indian chief.

The air inside the teepee had been transformed into a very hot substance that was thick with moisture and mint. The air was hard to breathe at first, but as Jacob took several deep breaths, he could feel his own lungs opening as he breathed normally, even though the heat from the fire and the several clay pots of boiling water made it uncomfortable to stay in the teepee long. Not liking to bear the heat any longer, he moved the hide cover aside so he could step back outside into the fresh air.

"Do you see now what has been created for the sick?" Brown Bear said once they were both outside.

"Yes, I do," Jacob admitted. "I hope it will help."

"I am confident it will," Brown Bear said. White Raven was coming out of the back of the clinic with a few Indian braves, a very concerned expression on his face. He spoke to Brown Bear then in their native language, and Jacob waited patiently for an explanation of what was being discussed.

"White Raven explains that another miner has died. They have been drugged so that they are forced to sleep and not allow their bodies to work out the sickness. There has also been much bloodletting," Brown Bear said to Jacob, his face pained with the news. "My warriors will begin to bring out those that are still alive and place them in the teepees. They will be stripped of their clothes, which will then be burned in the fire. They will remain till the sickness leaves them."

"I understand. I appreciate what you are doing for these men," Jacob said. "What of Rosa Casey? What of any women that have been affected by this cough?"

"Bring all that are sick. The women that are sick shall be tended to as well," Brown Bear said. Jacob nodded, hoping that no one else would be found sick.

"I'll go bring her right away." Jacob then left the back of the clinic just as the miners were brought out. None of them looked thrilled to being pulled out of the clinic by Indians, but they were in no condition to protest as they continued to cough hard. Jacob made his way round to the main street and into the inn. There he saw that several of the miners that stayed at the inn were huddled in the hallway outside of Rosa's room, looking in with concerned faces.

Jacob's heart thudded against his chest as he asked for them to clear the space. As he reached the room, he looked in to see Rosa in much the same condition as when he'd left her. Only now her face was flushed as though she was hot and her body seemed very weak as she continued to cough and did her best to cover her mouth.

"Oh, Jacob. Thank goodness you've returned. She's burning up," Mrs. Tibet looked up from Rosa's bedside. "Is Dr. Harvey on his way?"

"Dr. Harvey is as sick as the rest of them," Jacob explained. "Brown Bear and the other Sioux Indians have set up teepees outside the clinic and have come up with a way to deal with the cough." Mrs. Tibet's eyes widened at the mention of Indians.

"But what could Indians possibly do for sick people?" she asked.

"Please, Mrs. Tibet. You're going to have to trust me. I have already been inside one of the teepees and felt how it helps someone to breathe easier," Jacob pleaded. Mrs. Tibet didn't appear as though she was going to relent, but eventually she got up off the side of the bed, making room for Jacob. He pulled the bedlinen around Rosa, making her into a parcel he could carry.

"I'm at least coming with you," Mrs. Tibet decided. "Just to make sure she remains alright." Jacob wasn't going to argue with the older woman. He pulled Rosa into his good arm. As Jacob righted himself with her body close to his, he could feel heat radiating from her as though she had a fever. Yet the touch of her skin was very cold and clammy.

Jacob didn't waste any time. Rosa started to cough once more as they finally rounded the clinic and came upon the Indians. Jacob could hear others coughing from within the teepees, and as soon as Jacob appeared with Rosa, Brown Bear came to his side and guided him into the third teepee.

"We decided to leave this one just for women affected by the cough," Brown Bear explained and held back the flap so Jacob could move inside with Rosa in his arms. Inside were several Indian maidens working on coaxing up a large fire to boil the several clay pots of water and herbs. When Jacob came in, they were quick to help him lay Rosa on a pile of furs. She began to cough again and one of the Indian maidens was quick to come to her aid, helping her sit up as she coughed with all her might. Next, one of the maidens took a small jar from a bundle hanging from the top of the teepee and started opening the clothes around her chest.

"Come, Jacob," Brown Bear said. "They will need to remove her clothing for the medicine to take effect." Jacob looked at Rosa, staring at her weak form as she coughed in the arms of one of the Indian maidens. Her eyes never came open as she coughed and for a moment Jacob feared ever getting to see her beautiful brown eyes again.

"Go, Jacob. I will remain with her," Mrs. Tibet said. Jacob hadn't realized that the older woman had followed him into the teepee. He thought that it had to be Mrs. Tibet's first time in such a dwelling, but as Jacob looked down at the woman, she didn't hold any fear in her eyes of the Indians. She was only concerned about Rosa's wellbeing. Thinking that Mrs. Tibet could be the perfect motherly figure for Rosa, he relented and finally stepped out of the teepee with Brown Bear.

"Is my wife going to be okay in there, Jacob?" Mr. Tibet asked as the two came out.

"Probably the safest place in the world, Mr. Tibet. Brown Bear and his people are trustworthy Indians, I assure you," Jacob said as he placed a hand on the man's shoulder to comfort him.

"Are there any more that are sick?" Brown Bear asked as he looked around at the three teepees. White Raven had just come out of one of the teepees and was heading his way. The chief moved, eager to hear what his medicine man had to say. Jacob shook his head at the question.

After listening to White Raven, Brown Bear turned to Jacob. "Those afflicted are all prepared for the cleansing," he said. "White Raven will begin preparing a fire so that he may bless and pray for this cleansing to be successful."

Brown Bear looked closely at Jacob. "White Raven is going to perform his ceremony. He says that all are ready to be prayed over. We need to be certain there will be no interference." Jacob picked out his deputy in the throng around him and Brown Bear and they both nodded. "I'm thinking that any sort of prayers will be very beneficial at this point," Jacob said. Then he turned to the innkeeper. "Mr. Tibet, I don't think there is really anything else we can do here," Jacob said to the older man. "Why don't you head back home? I'll let you know if anything else happens with the women."

"I'm putting a lot of trust in you, Sheriff," Mr. Tibet said, giving Jacob a stern look and then turned away. Jacob watched him walk back to the inn, thinking that the weight on his shoulders had only become heavier.

"It will take some time, but this will work, Jacob," came Brown Bear's voice. It sounded comforting, but all Jacob could think about was the number of people that had already died. If this didn't work, he'd not only have a panicked town, but a lot of people who might turn their anger and fear towards the Sioux.

Jacob made his way through the small crowd to Tanner. He was standing with Edward James, both watching with critical eyes as everyone moved about. White Raven had finished preparing his bonfire with the help of a few other Indian braves, and as the fire rose, so did the medicine man's voice as he began to pray and sing.

His body moved to the sound of the song as he performed the ritual.

"Tanner, we better start making our rounds and let everyone know what is going on. I'm sure the entire town knows by now that there are a group of Indians behind the clinic. They're going to want to know why and what they are doing," Jacob said.

"That isn't a bad idea," Tanner replied, his eyes darting through the small camp as though he was nervous about what he was seeing. "I just hope all of this works."

"It will," Edward said in the same confident tone that Brown Bear had used a moment ago. Jacob watched as Edward and Tanner exchanged a look, one that seemed to calm the deputy for a moment.

"We'll be back in a bit," Jacob said as he looked at Edward. Then, with Tanner in tow, they started the long process of visiting with everyone in town to explain the situation and make sure that no one started to panic or cause any trouble for what Brown Bear and his people were working hard to accomplish.

CHAPTER 13

*R*osa was lost in the fog of her mind. She could still feel and hear everything around her even though she felt too exhausted to even open her eyes. All that she had energy left to do was cough when the tickle would come to the back of her throat. No matter how hard she tried to fight it, she couldn't stop herself from coughing and becoming weaker and weaker.

At one point after the sickness had claimed her, she realized she was being moved. She'd spent so much time in bed that she could tell when she'd been picked up by strong arms, arms that gave her a sense of being cared for, that were transporting her somewhere else. When she was settled again, she felt the heat of her body intensify. She became both hot on the inside and outside as her skin began to sweat. Only when her clothing had been removed did she feel any sort of comfort. Her skin was then enclosed in furs, and though she struggled to breathe every time the coughing began, at least her body felt more comfortable.

In the distance Rosa could hear someone singing. It was a rich voice that filled the air. She didn't understand what the words were, but she liked to focus her mind on it instead of the pain that filled her body. She was desperate to feel some sort of relief, to find a way to drive away the heat, but every time the coughing began once more, it seemed that the heat surrounding her was the only thing that helped her get through the coughing. Her mind focused on the sound of the song as it increased in volume and filled the air. Then her body focused on being able to cough up the substance that seemed to be stuck in her lungs.

Rosa didn't know how long it had been since she had been moved from the bed where her sickness had begun. She could tell she was somewhere else, somewhere much hotter where the air was thick with the smell of mint and moisture. It reminded Rosa of rainy days in the summer when the air became thick with moisture. But as time progressed, eventually the song she'd been so focused on died away along with her need to cough so frequently. Rosa even began to fall asleep, only occasionally being brought back to consciousness by the need to cough.

At one point, Rosa opened her eyes as though she'd suddenly woken up from a nightmare. Her body tensed as her eyes darted around the dark space. Rosa had no memory of where she was and why, as she turned her head to see a small fire burning beside her. Several clay pots rested on the embers, the sound of boiling water filling her ears. As she continued to look around, she found herself encircled by a strange texture that created the enclosure. She wanted to reach out and touch it to discover for herself what the material was, but as she lifted her arm, she looked down at her body to see that she was covered in furs, and that the furs were the only thing that she was wearing.

"What is going on?" Rosa asked in a soft voice. She turned her head back towards the fire as her eyes continued to adjust. Along the perimeter of the enclosure she was in, she saw several other mounds of furs and saw dark faces amongst them. Rosa had never seen an Indian before, but she could tell that the other women in the enclosure with her didn't quite look like anyone she'd ever seen. Finally she mustered up the strength to sit up.

Doing so was not a pleasant experience. Her body was stiff and exhausted from all the coughing. It was when her head stopped spinning that her body was overcome with the need to cough once more. Bringing her knees up to her chest, Rosa began to cough with all her might, spitting out the chunks of whatever was in her body as it was brought up from her lungs into her mouth. The sound of her coughing seemed to wake the others as several women sat up to look at her.

Arms came around her then and she quickly turned to see an Indian woman supporting her body as she coughed. Her eyes went wide as she looked at the woman, but the young lady only seemed to be concerned about her as she held Rosa up and began to pat her back. When the coughing was finished and Rosa spat out the contents of her mouth onto the grassy floor that surrounded her, the woman left her and moved over to the fire. Rosa watched with curiosity as the woman opened a pot and spooned out the contents into a small clay cup. Then, the woman returned to her side and handed the clay cup to Rosa.

Carefully, Rosa accepted the cup and looked inside. The water was dark and hot in her hands. She blew on it for a minute or two before trying how it tasted. The tea was very bitter, unlike the tea she was used to in Boston. But since her throat was so raw and scratchy, the hot liquid was a welcome relief.

"Where am I?" Rosa asked softly once she had finished drinking the tea. The Indian woman looked at her curiously. Rosa hadn't thought that the woman might not speak her language. So, she pointed to herself and said, "Rosa," before pointing at the woman. The woman didn't say anything in reply but continued to watch Rosa carefully. Rosa was beginning to worry about why she was with a bunch of Indian women, even though they seemed to be taking care of her.

Rosa looked towards the opening of the enclosure and watched as Mrs. Tibet appeared. Rosa felt immediately relieved to see a familiar face and smiled up at the older woman as she came near.

"Looks like someone is feeling better," Mrs. Tibet said as she sat down next to her on the ground.

"Mrs. Tibet, where on earth are we?" Rosa asked as she glanced at the Indian woman beside her. The other woman seemed to be watching her carefully, and Rosa wasn't sure how she felt about that.

"This is a teepee, Rosa," Mrs. Tibet explained. "Edward James and the Sheriff went up into the mountains to talk to the Sioux Indians. They came down from the mountain and set up all these teepees for those who were sick with the cough." Mrs. Tibet quickly covered her mouth then and coughed into her hands, making Rosa very concerned about the older woman.

"Oh no, not you, too," Rosa said as she placed her hand on the woman's shoulder.

"I'm feeling fine," Mrs. Tiber reassured her. "These Indians really know their stuff when it comes to treating sick people. I've been sitting in this teepee all afternoon and night, breathing in whatever they have boiling over the fire. And the salve for the chest is helping me cough up whatever is in my body."

"It's rather hot in here," Rosa observed as she looked around. "I feel like I'm burning up despite only being covered by furs."

"I don't really understand it myself, but it seems to be working. The miners that had been sick are in two other teepees and everyone's coughing seems to have gone down," Mrs. Tibet explained.

"Then can we return to the inn?" Rosa asked as she looked around. She wasn't particularly comfortable being surrounded by Indians she didn't know. More importantly, she wanted to be in normal clothes again.

"Jacob explained that it's best if we remain until the cough is completely gone," Mrs. Tibet said, bringing Rosa's attention back to her.

"But how long is that going to take?"

Mrs. Tibet sighed as she shook her head. "I don't know, but just seeing you awake makes me think that whatever they are doing is really working." Rosa knew she should be thankful for what the Indians were doing for her and the others that were sick. She simply wasn't that comfortable being in a teepee. Rosa did her best to remain grateful and optimistic. At least she had Mrs. Tibet with her even though she'd probably gotten the older woman sick in the process.

"Is there anything to eat?" Rosa asked, her stomach tight from not having eaten anything in a long time. Though her body hurt from all the coughing, she needed some nourishment for her exhausted body.

"Yes. The Indian women have prepared a thick soup that is mostly onion and garlic. It doesn't have a bad flavor, but the vegetables are very strong," Mrs. Tibet explained.

"Why just garlic and onion?" Rosa asked.

"It was explained to me by Edward James that these vegetables are very good for healing the inside of the body," Mrs. Tibet explained. "Would you like me to go get you a bowl? The soup is being kept warm over the fire outside." Rosa nodded, thinking that any food would be better than none. Mrs. Tibet left the teepee and Rosa took the time to look around her.

The Indian woman that had come to Rosa's aid when she'd first woken up was now tending to the fire in the teepee. She fed it with more logs and carefully opened the lids of all the clay pots full of boiling water. The woman then started to add more water to the pots from a large bucket that had been placed at the side. As she did this, the teepee seemed to grow warmer as the air thickened with moisture and mint. Rosa didn't like how it made her skin feel sticky, but as she took deep breaths, she felt herself being able to breathe easier.

After a while, Mrs. Tibet returned to the teepee carrying a small bowl of soup. She had to explain how the Indians didn't use forks or spoons, that she'd have to drink it from the side. Rosa didn't mind since she was so hungry. It didn't take her long to finish the bowl of soup even though the taste of onion and garlic was very strong. Being practically naked in a teepee full of other women didn't really cause Rosa to fear about her manners. The only thing she was concerned about was feeling better as soon as she could.

"Seems the only thing we have left to do is get some sleep," Mrs. Tibet spoke up after the Indian woman had come to them and put a strong-smelling salve on both their necks and upper chests. It smelled like peppermint and lavender, and already Rosa felt herself growing tired. The woman then washed her hands in the bucket of water and made her way over to a bundle of furs she'd been sleeping on.

"I suppose you are right," Rosa said as she eased herself down onto her own pile of furs. "Will you be okay sleeping in a teepee?" Mrs. Tibet chuckled as she eased herself down next to Rosa and pulled a few furs around her.

"I've slept in worse conditions," Mrs. Tibet replied. "It's nice and warm in here, and if whatever they're boiling in those pots is going to help this cough go away, I'm willing to sleep one night away from home."

"Thank you for staying with me," Rosa said as she yawned. When another coughing fit came through her body, Rosa was able to shield her mouth with her elbow and cough just once before the need left her. She could tell that whatever the Indians had chosen to do, it was working for her.

"No one deserves to be alone when they're sick," Mrs. Tibet replied with a kind smile. "It's quite like taking care of one of my children again."

Rosa felt what a motherly figure Mrs. Tibet was. How lucky she was to have found such a safe haven with the Tibets. Almost as lucky as Jacob Benning turning out to be such an attractive and caring man. For a moment Rosa wondered how Katelyn was surviving with a new lady's maid. Soon, though, both Rosa and Mrs. Tibet were fast asleep.

JACOB WOKE the next day wondering what was going to be facing him that morning. It had been rough talking to the townsfolk the day before. As expected, no one liked the idea of the Indians spending time in town. Normally every once in a while an Indian brave or Brown Bear would come into town and speak with either himself or to trade for goods at the mercantile. But since Mr. Fry wasn't the friendliest towards Indians, not many came to town unless it was rather important. On top of explaining why the Indians had set up teepees behind the clinic, once everyone started to hear the reason why, Jacob had to deal with a spreading panic amongst the people that they would also become sick and would be at the mercy of the Indians.

Between him and Tanner, it had taken the rest of the day to reassure everyone that as long as they stayed away from the clinic, they wouldn't get sick. A few even tried to explain to Jacob that the Sioux Indians were dangerous people and that those who were sick would only die if left in their care. But after Jacob started to threaten jail time to those who would try to interfere with the Indians, no one tried to convince him otherwise.

As night had fallen, Jacob decided to camp outside of Rosa's teepee. He wanted to be there just in case any of the town's people tried to start something in the middle of the night. But he also wanted to be close to Rosa in case she became afraid of being around Indians. At one point in the night, Mrs. Tibet had woken him to explain that Rosa was awake and feeling better. If Rosa had been properly dressed, he'd have gone to her immediately to see for himself that she was faring better. But Jacob understood what condition Rosa was in and instead watched as Mrs. Tibet fetched her a bowl of soup and returned to the teepee.

After that, Jacob had done his best to get comfortable on his bedroll in hopes of gaining just a few hours of sleep before dawn. It was when White Raven approached him that Jacob finally gave up on trying to get comfortable so he could sleep. He was just too worried to really sleep that night. And laying on the hard ground did little to ease the discomfort in his body from having his right arm in a sling all the time.

Then White Raven appeared by his side. Language difficulties made it too difficult to communicate with the Indian medicine man. Jacob just looked at him and waited to see what he wanted. There were white streaks of hair mixed in the long black strands, showing signs of age. Wrinkles framed his eyes and face, but as he smiled, his eyes held a sense of comfort that meant Jacob did not feel alarmed. Even as White Raven reached forward and started to inspect his right arm, Jacob did not worry but only watched the man with curious eyes.

As White Raven began to manipulate the muscles in Jacob's right shoulder, Jacob did his best to fight off the pain, hoping the man knew what he was doing.. The muscles were tight and sore, but the more White Raven moved his fingers and hands on them through Jacob's Western shirt, the more they felt better. At one point, White Raven reached into his pouch that he carried around his waist and revealed a small container. As he slid off the lid, Jacob could see an oily substance inside that White Raven then began to apply to his neck and shoulders. It was an odd sensation, but Jacob wasn't going to protest. He'd been in such pain for so long that he was willing to try anything. Jacob could then feel a strange heat on his skin where White Raven had applied the oil. It seemed to soothe his muscles much as a hot bath would.

After White Raven finished working on his shoulder, he handed Jacob the container and placed it inside his left hand, folding his fingers around it. Jacob figured that he was being given the oil and felt grateful to have something to put on his sore muscles every night. White Raven then took his right arm and very carefully slipped it out of the sling he constantly wore. Just having the pressure off his shoulder for a moment felt good, but Jacob was nervous about what White Raven was about to do with his plastered arm.

First, White Raven began to move the fingers of his right hand slowly. They poked out of the plaster and had very little movement to them, and the little movement that White Raven was causing his fingers to do seemed to really agitate his arm. It was like moving your leg for the first time in hours after you've sat for way too long at a desk. It was uncomfortable at first, but eventually it felt alright. White Raven did this for several minutes, making Jacob's arm feel like it was being moved for the first time in months. Eventually, White Raven finished what he was doing and placed his arm back in the sling. He then closed his eyes and began to speak in his language, his hands resting gently on his right shoulder and arm. Jacob simply watched, thinking that White Raven was praying over him at that moment.

When White Raven finished praying, he opened his eyes and gave Jacob a kind smile. He then rose and left him, traveling back across the camp and disappearing inside one of the teepees. Jacob didn't know what to think about the encounter, but he was very grateful for what White Raven had done for him and his arm. His shoulders even felt lighter, and as Jacob lay back down on his bedroll, he found himself able to relax and drift off to sleep.

CHAPTER 14

The next time Rosa opened her eyes, she could clearly see that it was daylight once more. The sun peeked in through the top of the teepee where the smoke from the fire escaped. Rosa turned her head slowly, seeing that the fire in the middle was still burning strongly. The air was still thick, but this time when Rosa sat up, she didn't feel the need to cough. She took several deep breaths, feeling like she'd slept for days and now had the energy to move freely.

Mrs. Tibet was no longer lying beside her, but the Indian women that had been sleeping the night before were now up and moving. Some tended to the fire while others filled the clay pots with water and herbs. As Rosa looked up, she could now see that several bundles were hanging down from the teepee poles, and the women seemed to be using their contents to put into the boiling pots of water. For several minutes, Rosa simply watched them work, thinking that she'd never seen anything so fascinating in her life.

Since Rosa had never seen an Indian before, she was interested to observe these women closely. Their tanned skin seemed to match perfectly with their long black hair that many had braided down their backs. Their dresses were made from what looked like deer hide, which was also what the teepee seemed to be constructed from. Underneath their gowns they wore leggings of some sort that were fastened with ties down their legs. Rosa had never considered wearing leggings before and wondered if they were as uncomfortable as they looked. But since Rosa was currently wearing nothing but fur pelts it was impossible to judge.

At one point, the Indian woman that had tended to her the previous night came back to her side and gave her another cup of tea. Once it had cooled a little, Rosa drank it all. She was curious to know what the tea had been made from because this cup tasted much better than the last one. She could taste hints of berry and thought that she'd be willing to enjoy it on several occasions. As Rosa looked at the women, she only wished that somehow she could talk to them and learn exactly what they were doing.

Eventually, Rosa was brought another bowl of soup. She kept watching the flap of the teepee, waiting for Mrs. Tibet to return. She wanted to speak with someone and learn about the condition of the other miners. And since Mrs. Tibet had been coughing last night, she wondered why the older women wasn't in the teepee with her. But Rosa's worries were temporarily distracted as the Indian woman who had been tending to her came to her side and handed her an Indian gown with leggings. At first, Rosa just looked down at the clothes, not sure what the woman wanted her to do. As Rosa looked up at her, she laughed at her and began to help Rosa into the clothes. Rosa found it all very strange but thought that any clothes would be better than none.

Rosa set the furs aside as she got dressed. Surprisingly, the gown and leggings were rather soft against her skin and didn't feel heavy at all. As the Indian woman helped her to her feet, she almost didn't feel like she was wearing anything at all as she used her left hand to feel the touch of the fabric over her skin. The Indian woman then had Rosa stand still while she braided her curly blonde hair. By the time the woman was finished, Rosa looked down at herself and wondered how much like an Indian she now looked.

Next, the woman led Rosa from the teepee, and as she stepped outside for the first time in what felt like forever, Rosa had to raise her hand and shield her sensitive eyes from the sunlight. She blinked a few times before she followed the Indian woman away from the teepee where the other maidens were now carrying the clay pots on long poles to the two other teepees that were set up near the back of the clinic.

Rosa had to stand still for a moment and really take in everything around her. She took several deep breaths, the air cool on her skin compared to the heated teepee. It felt refreshing as she struggled to keep her balance. She'd been so exhausted for so long while laying down that it almost felt uncomfortable to stand on her feet. Rosa watched as men, both white and Indian, moved around the camp. Some were coming in and out of the clinic while others sat around another bonfire.

Eventually the Indian woman that had been tending to Rosa looped arms with her and helped her walk over to the central fire. It was slow going as Rosa felt stiff all over, but she was glad that at least she was moving about. She was even more pleasantly surprised when she saw Jacob sitting with the other Indian men, looking a little worse for wear. But when their eyes met, his jaw dropped open as his eyes traveled up and down her body. Rosa blushed hard, worried about what Jacob would think of her in Indian clothing.

"You must be Rosa Casey," came a deep voice. Rosa turned her eyes and looked at the Indian man who had addressed her. She was surprised to see that he only wore leggings, that his upper torso was bare except for a very large and elaborate necklace that hung around his neck. Rosa made sure not to look at his bare skin as she instead looked deeply into his obsidian eyes. A large feather hung from his long black hair, making him appear intimidating. Yet, his eyes held a warmth that made Rosa curious about him.

"I am," Rosa replied, realizing only then that the man was speaking English with her and asking if she was Miss Casey.

"My name is Brown Bear," the man added, making it clear to Rosa with whom she was speaking. She remembered his name, and then remembered that this Indian was in fact the chief of the Sioux Indians in the mountains.

"Thank you," Rosa said then, trying to think of a better response. "I have very much appreciated all the help I've been given to feel better." Brown Bear smiled at her. 'I like that you are so polite even though I can see that all these Indians frighten you. Being able to help all these sick people is our pleasure. I do not like the idea of anyone dying if I have the power to prevent it. And, I have learned that you are to be Jacob's intended." Rosa's blush deepened as her eyes drifted to Jacob. He was watching her intensely and for that moment Rosa wished to be in a normal gown instead of the light fabric of the Indian dress.

"If all goes well," Rosa said and dipped her head towards the Chief. Then she made her way over to Jacob and sat beside him on the log, eager to be no longer the center of attention. The Indian woman that had been tending to Rosa then began to speak with her chief in their native language, giving Rosa the opportunity to just sit and breathe.

"How are you feeling?" Jacob eventually said. He hadn't expected Rosa to be dressed like an Indian maiden. The clothing she wore was rather fitting and highlighted her beautiful form. Her curly hair had been tamed into a braid, making Jacob mistakenly assume she was another Indian maiden until he'd looked up at her and into her brown eyes. Seeing her awake was such a relief that seeing her in her current outfit had taken him completely by surprise.

"I am feeling much better, thank you," Rosa answered. "Is Mrs. Tibet feeling well? I have not seen her this morning."

"Yes, it seems her cough was very short lived. She returned back to the inn this morning."

"And what about the other miners? I don't hear anyone coughing any longer."

"They are still resting in the teepees, they need time to make a full recovery. But Dr. Harvey is up and moving." Rosa nodded, thinking that was all rather good news. She'd only been sick for one full day, but it had been enough to show her how hard it would have been to be sick for several days. She certainly understood why men had died from the terrible cough.

"If you want, I can escort you back over to the inn so you can finish resting there. I can have Dr. Harvey come check on you if you think the cough is returning," Jacob offered.

"I'm okay for the moment," Rosa said. "I'll return to the inn today, but for now I just want to take things slowly." Jacob nodded, trying to see things through Rosa's perspective. He watched her carefully, relieved that she was up and moving around. Just seeing her eyes open let Jacob know that she was feeling much better.

An Indian maiden came and gave Rosa a plate of food. Rosa looked down at the plate, seeing something that looked similar to a gruel next to a small stack of flat bread. She smiled at the woman as she walked away, and then turned to Jacob wondering if he could tell her what it was she had been given to eat.

"It's a mixture made from ground corn and hot water. They have flavored it and added plenty of garlic and onions," Jacob explained. "You're supposed to use your fingers and use the bread to scoop it up and eat it."

"This is quite different than anything I've ever done before," Rosa admitted. "And I think the Indians really like their onions and garlic." Jacob chuckled, seeing how Rosa could think that.

Rosa experimented with using the bread almost as a spoon and taking a small bite of the mixture. She found it pleasing enough and made sure to eat all of what she'd been given. Once she felt better, she'd be back in the kitchen with Mrs. Tibet and they'd be able to cook whatever they wanted.

"It's really good to see you doing better," Jacob said once Rosa had finished eating. He was so overcome with so many emotions of relief that he was doing his best not to overwhelm anyone else with them. Rosa looked up at Jacob and thought she saw tears in his eyes. He did look tired and she wondered if he'd been sick as well.

"I'm sure I have you to thank for my recovery," Rosa said with a smile. "I see that the Indians are the ones that brought the teepees and knew what to do, but I do have a distant memory of someone carrying me into the teepee." Jacob smiled at her, thinking how nice it had been to hold her close and that he'd like to do that again some-time soon.

"My part was only a small one," Jacob admitted. "I just kept the peace." Rosa nodded, thinking that that had probably been no small matter, then that it was about time she returned to the inn.

"How do I thank all of them?" Rosa asked as she looked at the Indi-ans. "They have helped save the lives of complete strangers. And I bet some of them, if not all the miners, aren't big at being around Indians."

"Actions speak louder than words," Jacob said. "I think you could thank all of them personally, but perhaps we can think of some other way to thank them."

"We?" Rosa asked, a small smile coming to her lips. Jacob looked down at her, realizing his error. But he thought it was fitting since he really wanted to work hard now to court Rosa properly. He'd come close to losing her and he didn't want to take any more chances when it came to their future.

"Yes, we," Jacob repeated. "I'm sure it will be easier to come up with something special together." Rosa's smile grew brighter as she thought the idea was fitting. Now that she was feeling better, she realized how much she wanted to spend time with Jacob and really get to know him. She wanted to feel more comfortable with the idea of marrying him. She knew that he was brave and willing to help anyone. But she wanted to know for sure that he'd be the perfect match for her.

Jacob helped Rosa to her feet and together they thanked Brown Bear profusely. The Indian chief gratefully accepted their apprecia-tion and wished Rosa better health in the future. As Jacob led her away from the camp behind the clinic, Rosa realized she had felt safe around the Indians even though it had been surprising to see these natives for the first time. She was also looking forward to being back at the inn and in some more comfortable clothing.

The moment Rosa stepped into the inn, she was greeted warmly by everyone. Jacob was surprised to see that so many people had come to the inn and wondered if this was where everyone in town had been spending their time since the Indians had arrived. Jacob thought that he might have to act quickly to maintain good order. Yet, everyone only seemed interested in seeing Rosa and making sure she was okay.

"Oh, my dear, I was so worried about you," Mr. Tibet said as he gave Rosa a warm hug. "When Mrs. Tibet came home this morning, I was so concerned about you."

"Don't worry, Mr. Tibet. The Indians were very kind and attentive. I hope to repay the kindness of the Indian women who tended me the whole time I was recovering. I know that it was their method that cured me and all the others who had been affected by that terrible cough," Rosa said proudly. She truly was thankful for the Indians and wanted others to know that the Sioux were actually kind people. Mr. Tibet looked at her wearily, not appearing to be too convinced.

"Well, you two come in and get something to eat. I've been cooking all morning since I didn't have much to do while we waited," Mrs. Tibet said as she guided the couple into the dining room. Rosa didn't have the heart to say she wasn't hungry, and thankfully Jacob was quick to come to her rescue.

"Mrs. Tibet, I'm sure Rosa would like to change into something more comfortable for her and perhaps lay down for a bit," Jacob spoke up. "She is only just up." Rosa could have kissed the man since she dearly wanted to at least change into a different outfit.

"Oh, yes. Of course, my dear," Mrs. Tibet said as she looked and realized how Rosa was dressed. Rosa thanked those who had wished her good health as she parted ways and went to her bedroom. Once the door was closed, Jacob turned his attention to the small crowd.

"So, looks like the inn is pretty busy today," Jacob said loudly, gathering everyone's attention. A few looked at Jacob warily, like Mr. Fry and the Mayor, who couldn't quite meet his eyes. Jacob wasn't afraid to address a small crowd, especially when his gut feeling told him that someone was up to trouble.

"We'd just come to hear from Mrs. Tibet herself how she'd been treated," Mr. Fry spoke up. "And it's a relief that Miss Casey made it out of there alive."

"Mr. Fry, there is no reason for anyone to think that Brown Bear and his people would ever cause us any harm. It was him and his people that just saved over ten lives when this cough couldn't even be cured by our good doctor," Jacob said, addressing the entire crowd. Several other businessmen were present and he figured he'd only have to say this once since so many people were together.

"If it wasn't for Edward James coming up with the idea to speak to Brown Bear about what could be done for the many sick miners and even Miss Casey, there would be plenty more dead right now. The sickness spreads quickly and it wouldn't have taken but a few days for everyone in town to have become very sick. It's a cough that takes your breath away till you die. We should be very grateful that the Sioux Indians just saved this town from total destruction."

After Jacob had finished speaking, the room fell very quiet. No one could lift their eyes and look at him. They knew that what the Sheriff was talking about was true. They felt wrong for accusing the Indians of being malicious, even though they were sure they'd never be able to trust an Indian with their own lives. One by one, those that had gathered started to leave the inn until it was only Mr. and Mrs. Tibet left in the dining room with the other miners that rented rooms at the inn.

Mrs. Tibet eventually spoke up and said, "Come, fix your plates. No point letting good food go to waste." And with that, everyone filed into the kitchen to eat the good food that Mrs. Tibet had made that day.

CHAPTER 15

*A*s the days passed after Rosa returned to the inn, things in Bear Creek seemed to return to normal. After two more days, the Indians returned to the mountains with all of their belongings. While most of the town's people had stayed clear of the area behind the clinic, several others had come forward to thank Brown Bear personally. Rosa and Mrs. Tibet had cooked everyone a meal one night, and though Mr. Tibet didn't invite the Indians to dine at the inn, Rosa convinced him to at least help carry the food over to the teepees so that the miners could have a good meal. He was then able to see for himself that the miners were getting better and that no one had died since the Indians had first come down to help the town.

The best part of getting back to a normal routine was the time Rosa was spending with Jacob. Finally she was able to watch the sunset with him as they walked to the top of the hill outside of town. Rosa loved watching the sunset, thinking it was the prettiest she'd ever seen. It was great to have enjoyed the experience with Jacob and she hoped that they would be able to spend many unique experiences like this together in the future.

Jacob felt very much the same way as Rosa did. It was nice that things in Bear Creek were returning to some sort of normalcy. Jacob didn't have to worry about anyone else getting sick or dying because of the cough. Once Dr. Harvey had gotten better, he had most of the things at the boarding house taken out and either deeply cleaned or burned. The miners that lived there didn't know whom to pay their rent to since Mr. Cricket had passed away and so far no one had come to town to claim the business. Therefore, Mayor Franklin had stepped up to start managing the boarding house with the help and guidance of Mr. Tibet. Together, the two men really started to change the place around, giving each miner their own room and putting certain rules in place to ensure the place was kept clean and free of sickness. Those miners who had barely been able to keep their lives and recover from the cough were eager to obey any of the rules as long as they didn't get sick again.

Jacob was certain that everything in town was going to move forward as it should. He was getting time with Rosa between the meals she cooked with Mrs. Tibet. Sometimes they just took long walks together, talking about their plans for the future or what it was like to grow up in different parts of the country. He was really starting to think that sometime soon he should propose to Rosa and hoped that she would be ready to make things official between them.

A Saturday, two weeks after she had recovered from the coughing sickness, Rosa had finally made time to take her trunk down to the bank to make her big deposit. With everything that had happened since she'd first came to Bear Creek, Rosa had completely forgotten about putting all her money in the bank. She'd been comfortable with keeping it close to her, but since she couldn't keep watch over her things all day while she was working in the kitchen, she figured that now was the best time to do so.

As Rosa walked down the road that morning carrying her large portmanteau, Jacob spotted her from across the road as he was making his way to the clinic. He'd planned on paying Dr. Harvey a visit and talking to him about getting the plaster off his arm. He'd been using the oil that White Raven had given him and moved his fingers in about the same way to get his arm to exercise a little more. There was no doubt he had much more movement with it and thought it was about time the plaster could come off. Then he'd start using the arm a little bit more each day. But once he saw Rosa walking up the street with her trunk in her hand, Jacob's heart dropped. He was terrified that she was leaving town all of a sudden and he couldn't let that happen.

Jacob dashed across the road, paying no attention to any traffic and almost collided with a group of horses as four men rode into town. Jacob apologized as he dodged the group and continued on his way. He called out to Rosa. She looked round and smiled at him. Jacob thought that if she was willing to smile at him like that then perhaps she wasn't planning to do what he thought she was.

"Good morning, Jacob," Rosa greeted him happily. She thought that the best part of living in a small town was that she got to see Jacob almost every day unexpectedly. But as she looked into his eyes, she saw that he looked very worried, frightened almost. "Are you okay?"

Jacob swallowed hard as he ran his fingers through his hair. "Yeah. Umm, where are you going with your trunk?" he asked, trying to act casual. He was breathing hard from dashing across the street and almost being trampled by a group of horses.

"Oh, I'm just headed to the bank to make a deposit is all," Rosa explained. "Why you look like you've seen a ghost!"

Jacob sighed heavily, feeling like he could breathe again. He'd jumped to conclusions and now would have to answer for his erratic behavior.

"Forgive me, Rosa. I was headed to the clinic to get my arm checked out by Dr. Harvey to see if I can get the plaster off. I saw you walking up the road with your trunk and I was afraid you'd decided to leave town."

At first, Rosa was surprised that Jacob would think she'd ever just up and leave, and as she realized how much that thought had affected him, she couldn't help but begin to laugh. Eventually, Jacob joined her. He knew that he'd been foolish and was just glad that Rosa could laugh at his funny behavior and that they could laugh together.

"Don't worry, Jacob. If I ever decided to leave Bear Creek, you'd be

A FAITHFUL BRIDE FOR THE WOUNDED SHERIFF

the first to know. And it would have been for an emergency," Rosa said, hoping to comfort him. "Why don't you escort me to the bank and then I'll join you over at the clinic?" Jacob smiled as he nodded.

"And you let me carry that for you," he said, taking hold of her portmanteau with his left hand. For a moment it looked as though she was going to protest, then she smiled and moved with him towards the bank. Once they reached it, he handed her back the case and opened the door for her with his left arm, cursing the fact he still only had one working arm.

"Good morning, Sheriff. Miss Casey," Mr. Fritz greeted them as they came into the bank. "How can I help you two?"

"I've come to make a deposit," Rosa said as she set her trunk on the counter. Mr. Fritz smiled at her as he helped her position the trunk and then when Rosa opened it, both men looked inside and stared to see that it was empty. Mr. Fritz's brows furrowed together until Rosa started to pull on the trunk's fabric. It eventually came lose, revealing the small fortune that Rosa had saved and brought with her to Bear Creek.

"Very clever, Miss Casey," Mr. Fritz said as he helped Rosa set stacks of dollar bills on the counter till Rosa had revealed all the money she'd been saving. Once that process was done, she closed the trunk and set it down at her feet so that the counter would be cleared.

Jacob watched the process fascinated. He'd had no idea Rosa had such wealth. It was surprising and a little intimidating. What kind of life did Rosa want to live with this much money? They'd talked about their future and at no point did Jacob ever feel that Rosa wanted a life more than he could have ever planned to give her.

"It will take me some time to count everything and put an official number in the ledger. You are more than welcome to wait or I can bring you a certificate later on in the day?" Mr. Fritz offered.

"The total should be three thousand even, Mr. Fritz. Not to say you're not honest, but I figure it might help in making the official count," Rosa explained. She eyed Jacob nervously, hoping she didn't give him the wrong impression. This was the money she'd saved over the years, combined with the severance pay she'd had from Mr.

Trevino and the generous gift that Katelyn had given her when she left Boston. Rosa figured that this savings could come in handy one day.

"I don't think we'll find any discrepancies when it comes to the total amount. Once I create your certificate, we can discuss the options for either keeping your money here at this bank, or the larger bank in Denver," Mr. Fritz said with a comforting smile. He'd also have to talk to her about his fee for keeping her money safe but would wait to discuss that once the official total had been determined.

"Thank you, Mr. Fritz. I look forward to speaking with you later in the day," Rosa said as she reached down to pick up her trunk. She smiled at Jacob and turned towards the door just as four men entered. Rosa figured she'd get out of their way so they could also do business with Mr. Fritz since from the soil that lined their fingers and face, they had to be miners bringing nuggets of gold. But Jacob grabbed her arm and pulled her back towards him. She looked at him, startled, then saw Mr. Fritz frantically stashing her money under the counter and feeling for something there.

"That's enough moving there," the man in the front of the group said as he quickly pulled out his pistol and fired towards Mr. Fritz. Rosa cried out, dropped her trunk and turned towards Jacob. He pushed her behind him and backed up, his eyes swiftly assessing the scene.. He'd been so focused on everyone who was so sick that he'd completely forgotten about the bank robbers the Marshall had telegrammed him about. Now he'd been caught unprepared.

Jacob looked at Mr. Fritz. The pistol shot had done no more than tear a hole in the sleeve of his smart jacket and the bank manager slowly raised his hands up. His gaze met Jacob's for a moment and Jacob shook his head, trying to tell Mr. Fritz to not do anything for the moment.

The group of bank robbers came forward. Jacob counted four men, all looking a little worse for wear. Their clothes were tattered and patched over and over while their hands and face were grimy as though they were miners. Jacob's mind started to race as he thought about how he was going to defend the bank and all the money Rosa had just brought into it.

Rosa was backed up against the wall. She didn't know what to do against four men with pistols. They all looked menacing. The one in the back, the tallest of the group, looked at her, his eyes arrogant, his hair greasy and black. When he smiled at her, a sickening feeling filled Rosa and she had to fight to keep her composure before she lost her wits and the breakfast she'd had that morning.

"Now hand over all the cash you have," said the man at the front of the group as he approached Mr. Fritz, his pistol aimed at the bank manager's torso. "No funny business or I won't hesitate to kill you." Jacob swallowed hard thinking that this man had to be desperate. But judging by their condition, it seemed that they were all a bit desperate.

"Money's locked up in the safe. Requires two keys and the other banker is not in right now," Mr. Fritz said smoothly. "You might just as well leave." The leader smirked, crooked and yellow teeth showing from behind thin lips. Mr. Fritz narrowed his eyes at the man. Jacob knew he was waiting to see what the robber would do next.

"I saw you put plenty of money underneath that counter," snarled the robbers' leader. "Let's start with that, and then perhaps one of my men can accompany you to this safe of yours."

"Yeah! Let's get the cash. We don't need the sheriff to turn up."

"Fast in and fast out, isn't that our motto?" said another of the robbers. They all looked restless and wanted their leader to get on with things..

Jacob looked at Mr. Fritz and could tell he was thinking if he agreed to give them the cash he could reach for the shotgun and get a shot off, clearing a way for Jacob and Rosa at least to escape. Jacob stared at him hard, urging him to forget such a reckless move and just comply with the robbers' instructions. He didn't want anyone dead, and if someone outside the bank had heard the gun fire, then perhaps help was already on the way.

Jacob inwardly cursed himself for getting his arm broken. His pistol still hung on his left hip in its holster, hidden by his vest. If his arm wasn't covered in plaster and in a sling, he could manage to reach it and fire off a shot creating a diversion that would be enough to distract the robbers and give Mr. Fritz time to pull out his shotgun. As it was even if he managed to get the gun out of the holster, he wouldn't be able to fire it. The sling did give him one advantage, though. The robbers could have no idea he was the sheriff, they would not see him as any danger. All he needed was for something unexpected to happen.

The bank robber waved his pistol at the bank manager. "Get on with it or you get it."

Suddenly the bank's door was opened, triggering the bell. All the robbers looked round as Margret Phillips came into the bank with her cleaning supplies. She gasped as she saw the gunmen - and fainted on the spot. Rosa screamed.

Jacob went for it. With his left hand, clumsily, he drew the pistol and fired instinctively. One of the robbers fell to the floor, blood pouring from his chest.

The robbers turned on him and raised their weapons..

Jacob knew he was a goner. He had no time to aim and fire again and get three men. He raised his gun to try for another robber, blinking, his breath frozen in his chest as he prepared for bullets to rip through his torso. Instead, just when he thought he was about to feel the pains of death, Mr. Fritz succeeded in pulling his shotgun out from underneath the counter and fired both barrels at the robbers. Two more fell. Jacob fired again. The last robber standing sank to his knees then keeled over.

WHEN JACOB'S ears stopped ringing from gun blast, he slowly lowered his pistol and peered around the bank as Mr. Fritz came around the counter reloading his shotgun. But the robbers lay bleeding and dying from being hit at such a close range by the shotgun. Jacob's last shot had lodged in the upper thigh of the fourth robber. It had struck an artery and he lay groaning with his life ebbing away. Satisfied by the damage, Mr. Fritz placed his gun on the counter and quickly went to the aid of Mrs. Phillips. She groaned and opened her eyes. The manager lifted her into his arms and carried her outside saying he'd take her to the clinic.

Jacob pulled Rosa to her feet and shielded her eyes from the massacre as he guided her out of the bank. People had started to spill out onto the street as they heard the shots. Now they crowded around the bank to see what had happened. When Jacob came stumbling out with Rosa, hands reached forward to help them both.

"What's happened, Sheriff?" asked Mr. Fry.

"Robbers, Mr. Fry," Jacob replied. "They're taken care of now, but I'm going to take Rosa to the clinic just in case." Mr. Fry let go of him then and helped Jacob lead Rosa over to the clinic. She hadn't spoken a word and Jacob was worried that she was in some sort of shock from the terrifying experience.

As they entered the clinic, they saw Mr. Fritz kneeling on the floor with Margret as Dr. Harvey administered smelling salts. It only took a second for Margret to come to as she looked around in a daze. Mr. Tibet shut the door behind them as Jacob kept his Rosa tucked under his left arm. He looked down at her and she continued to stare into the space before her without really focusing on anything.

"My goodness, what is going on?" Margret asked as Mr. Fritz helped her back onto her feet. He kept an arm around her, steadying her as she regained her balance.

"You fainted, Mrs. Phillips," Mr. Fritz said in a tender voice. Jacob eyed him, watching how he looked at Margret with concerned eyes. It made him wonder if the bank owner had feelings for the woman. "The bank was robbed and, unfortunately, you arrived to clean the bank at the most inopportune time."

"Explains why I feel sore all over," Margret replied as she looked around her. "Is Rosa alright?"

"Not sure," Jacob said as he looked at Dr. Harvey. The doctor came over to Rosa then and started to examine her. He placed both hands on either side of her face and looked deeply into her eyes as they continued to remain unfocused.

"Seems she's a little shocked by it all," Dr. Harvey said. "Did she witness the whole thing?" Jacob nodded once, feeling terrible for

Rosa. Jacob was used to the aftermath of a battle, so it no longer affected him. But he was now worried how seeing four men gunned down would forever affect Rosa.

"Have her take a seat over here," Dr. Harvey instructed. Jacob eased Rosa down into a wooden chair as Dr. Harvey went over to his medical bag and grabbed the smelling salts. "I need to get Rosa back to reality before there is any permanent damage," he said softly to Jacob. Jacob knelt beside Rosa and held her hand as she sat in the chair seemingly unaware of anything going on around her. He watched as Dr. Harvey came over to Rosa with a small, glass bottle and held it underneath her nose. It remained there until Rosa started to look around the room frantically as though she'd just woken up.

"Is everyone okay?" Rosa quickly asked as she clasped both hands on Jacob's. She looked down into his eyes, hers filled with worry and fear.

"Yes, Rosa. Everyone is fine. We're at the clinic now to have you checked out," Jacob explained.

Rosa looked down at her body, remembering hearing shots and afraid that she had sustained a wound. But after she had a good look at herself, she realized she was fine.

"What happened to me?" Rosa asked. She looked up and saw Dr. Harvey and some others from the town.

"You were in a state of shock for a short while," Dr. Harvey explained. "It's no surprise after what you witnessed." Rosa went silent then as she tried to remember what had happened. She thought about how the bank robbers had come into the bank, how Mrs. Phillips had entered the bank and distracted them just long enough for Jacob to fire his pistol and for Mr. Fritz to get hold of his shotgun. As the memory came back, so did her emotions during the whole thing. Tears welled up in her eyes as her body began to tremble. She gripped harder onto Jacob as she processed it all.

"I was so afraid I was going to lose you," Rosa sobbed as she looked at Jacob. "I thought for sure I was about to watch you die in front of me and then I'd never be able to tell you how much I've come to love you."

Jacob was stunned by Rosa's declaration of affection. At first, he didn't know what to say or do as Rosa continued to sob. But then he smiled as he stood and pulled Rosa to her feet. He then held her close to him, allowing her to cry into his chest as he rubbed her back with his left hand.

"I love you, too," Jacob said after a few moments. He'd never felt this way towards any woman before and he wanted her to feel assured that her feelings would be readily returned.

"You do?" Rosa whispered as she lifted up her head to look searchingly at Jacob. She hadn't planned on Jacob saying those words to her. She had simply wanted to express her love for him and to see if one day he would return her feelings. To hear him say those words so soon truly surprised her.

"When I first saw you step off that stagecoach, I thought you were the most beautiful woman I have ever seen. And after these few weeks you've been in Bear Creek, you've shown me that you are as beautiful on the inside as you are on the outside. You've become such a wonderful helper to Mrs. Tibet, and I can tell you enjoy working with her as well. And even though I'm sure it was a bit frightening at first, you've really warmed to Brown Bear and his people.

"It was when I was faced with the reality that I might lose you to that sickness, that I knew just how much I'd come to really care for you. My heart grieved over the chance of never being able to tell you just how much I love you. There isn't a single reason why any man in their right mind wouldn't fall head over heels for you, just like I have."

Rosa looked up into Jacob's eyes, stunned by his declaration. She was so overcome with his love that she couldn't help herself as she pressed herself onto her tiptoes and placed a quick kiss to his cheek. Rosa heard someone whistle behind them and she was instantly reminded that they weren't standing in the clinic alone. She blushed deeply as she chuckled, turning her gaze towards the others in the room.

"Nothing better than a romance," Mrs. Phillips said with a bright smile. "Mathew and Jenny are going to love this one."

"Alright then," Jacob said, a bit sheepishly. "There is a mess over at the bank. Mrs. Phillips, Mr. Fry. Would you see that Rosa gets back to the inn without any trouble? I want to get matters taken care of so no one else gets spooked."

"Sure thing, Sheriff," Mr. Fry said with a wink as he came forward and placed Rosa's arm on his. Jacob stepped back, thinking if he didn't need to go take care of the bank robbers that he'd love to spend the rest of the day with Rosa as they explored their newfound love for each other. But Jacob reminded himself that there would be plenty of time for that once things got settled again.

Mrs. Phillips thanked Mr. Fritz for all his help and then looped arms with Rosa before they left the clinic. Rosa looked over her shoulder and gave Jacob a bright smile before she was led away. Now that it was just the three men, Jacob took a deep breath and focused on the matter at hand.

"Dr. Harvey, if you wouldn't mind going to gather Curtis or Mitchel to help bring out the bodies, I'd appreciate it. Mr. Fritz, it might take some time to get the bank cleaned up, but I suppose you should secure everything before we invite anyone else inside to help out," Jacob said, remembering that Rosa's money was still tucked underneath the counter in the bank. Both men nodded as they all headed outside.

A small group of people still remained outside the bank. A few were trying to peer in through the door as whispers were heard all around. Jacob was a bit frustrated that so many people seemed to be nosey, but he couldn't blame them when it was easy to become spooked or scared when gunfire filled the small town.

"Alright folks, the bad guys were taken care of. How about you move along so we can take care of things?" Jacob called over the crowd. They all turned to face him, and after a moment, began to leave the street and step away from the bank. Tanner came jogging over, looking around with curiosity.

"Everything okay?" Tanner asked in a soft voice. Jacob chuckled as he pointed to the bank with his left hand.

"Four robbers entered the bank this morning. I was inside with Rosa and Mr. Fritz. Let's just say for now that the robbers are no longer a problem and no one else sustained an injury," Jacob explained. Tanner was shocked as he looked at the bank. "Help Dr. Harvey with the bodies," said Jacob. "I have a telegram to go send."

"You got it," Tanner said and joined Dr. Harvey and Mr. Fritz as they headed inside the bank.

Jacob sighed heavily as he made his way over to the mercantile. It would be good news about the robbers that he was sending over to the Marshall. He just hated that Rosa had to witness it all. As soon as he finished up his work, he'd be paying the woman he loved a visit.

CHAPTER 16

*R*osa was in a daze for the rest of the day. She helped Mrs. Tibet in the kitchen in the hopes of clearing her mind. She was still frightened by the memories of what she'd witnessed in the bank. Yet, she was also delighted about the fact that Jacob had returned her feelings. The thought that Jacob had fallen in love with her was enough to help keep the bad memories away while she worked.

"Don't know how much longer we'll be using the stove and oven if the days keep warming up like this," Mrs. Tibet said while they sliced steaks from the section of beef Mr. Tibet had purchased that morning. They'd roasted it in the oven all day and were now cutting small slices for the patrons that evening. It would be served with mashed potatoes, gravy, biscuits, and roasted vegetables. The smells were heavenly to Rosa and she thought how nice it would be to cook a large dinner for her family one day. She was envisioning being married to Jacob when she realized that Mrs. Tibet had spoken to her.

"We could cook the meat at night and serve it cold with pickled vegetables like cucumber and celery," Rosa suggested.

"That's certainly an idea. I was just thinking about making salted meat pastries. What other ideas do you have for the warmer weeks?"

Mrs. Tibet asked. Rosa always enjoyed it when Mrs. Tibet asked her opinion. The woman might have been cooking the same things for decades, but she was always willing to learn something new as well.

As Rosa and Mrs. Tibet discussed possible menu ideas that didn't require the stove or oven, Mr. Tibet came into the kitchen towards the end of dinner time to let Rosa know that Jacob had come to pay her a visit. She hadn't been expecting him and was excited about seeing him. She felt a bit nervous now that she knew that he loved her, but even more thrilled that he'd come that evening. After excusing herself from the kitchen when Mrs. Tibet reassured her that she could handle the rest, Rosa made her way into the dining room.

"Hi there," Rosa said as she came into the room. Jacob turned to face her from where he'd been standing near a window, gazing out at the town. He smiled as he looked at her, relieved about finding time that day to spend with her after everything that had happened. Jacob examined her closely, looking for signs of shock or depression. But the warm smile that Rosa shared with him was genuine and helped him relax in knowing that she was doing okay.

"Mr. Fritz asked me to deliver this to you," Jacob said as he handed her the bank certificate. Rosa took it and began to read the writing. She hadn't expected Mr. Fritz to find time to take care of her deposit today after everything that had happened that morning. But as she looked down at the certificate made out in her name with the exact amount of three-thousand dollars, she sighed with relief to know that it was officially deposited.

"Thank you for bringing this to me. It's a relief to know that my money has been deposited and is safe at the bank," Rosa said.

"And it's a relief to me to see you doing so well after such a terrible morning," Jacob admitted. Rosa gave him a smile as she nodded.

"I will agree that it was awful and that it will take some time for me to forget those horrible things. But knowing that you care about me is what kept me going all day." Rosa looked up into Jacob's beautiful blue eyes and watched as they shined at her as he smiled.

"I more than just care about you, Rosa. I truly love you," Jacob said. He came close to her then and pressed his lips lightly to her forehead.

Rosa closed her eyes, relishing the soft kiss. Then, when she opened her eyes, she watched as Jacob knelt before her. She was surprised as Jacob reached inside his vest with his left hand and pulled out a small ring from the inside pocket. He held it up towards Rosa for her to see the silver band with a single blue gemstone in it.

"Rosa Casey, I never knew that I was capable of loving someone as I've come to love you. I'm always looking forward to our time together, and every time you talk about your wants and dreams, all I want to do is see them come true. I want to be your husband and the father of all the children we both want. Rosa, I hope you'll make me the happiest man in the world and agree to be my wife."

Rosa placed a hand over her mouth as she looked at Jacob with wide eyes. She was so excited that she didn't move at first. Eventually her senses returned to her and she began to nod up and down as she fought back the happy tears.

"I'd be delighted to be your wife, Jacob," Rosa eventually said as she lowered her hands. A bright smile crossed Jacob's face as he slid the ring onto Rosa's finger, moving slowly as to not drop the delicate piece. Then he stood and wrapped his arms around Rosa the best he could with his right arm in a sling as he tried to express all his deep love for this wonderful woman.

"Come, let's go tell Mr. and Mrs. Tibet," Rosa suggested. She was so excited that she could hardly contain herself. And since the older couple had become like second parents to her, she wanted them to be the first ones to know. Jacob nodded as he allowed Rosa to take his hand and lead him into the kitchen. There, Mr. and Mrs. Tibet shared in their joy as Rosa showed them the ring and they praised them with much congratulations.

"Oh, it will be so nice to attend a late spring wedding. Just think of all the flowers we could gather for the special day," Mrs. Tibet exclaimed. "And we shall host such a wonderful reception at the inn. The dining room is plenty big enough."

"You are too kind," Rosa replied with a bright smile. She loved how excited the older woman was becoming over the idea of a wedding. It would be nice to have help in planning the big day. But as the older couple continued to chat excitedly about wedding plans, Rosa looked to Jacob and instead saw her entire future with such a wonderful man.

～

Dear Katelyn,

I have wonderful news. Jacob has asked me to marry him and I said yes. The wedding will be in a few weeks, as soon as Mrs. Fry can help me finish my wedding dress. I don't know if this letter will arrive before the day, but I wanted to let you know that I am happy and well in Bear Creek. Thank you for encouraging me to come out here because it's truly been the best thing I've ever done.

All my love,
Rosa

She had just finished writing her letter to Katelyn when a knock sounded on Rosa's bedroom door at the inn. It was about midafternoon, between the times when Rosa was needed in the kitchen to help with the evening meal. It was the part of the day that Rosa had a bit of time to herself, so as she quickly folded up her letter with the hopes of posting it, she opened up the door and was completely shocked by who was standing there.

"Katelyn! What are you doing here?" Rosa exclaimed as she came forward and wrapped her arms around her friend. But as she held Katelyn tightly to her, she realized that Katelyn had put on some serious weight. She leaned back and looked down at Katelyn's body, realizing that it wasn't just weight Katelyn had gained, she was pregnant.

"When Mama found out, she threatened to disown me. Then, Fredrick refused to acknowledge that he was the father and turned me away," Katelyn said as tears filled her eyes. "So I took what money I could get my hands on and came here. The very nice man at the mercantile told me where I could find you."

"Oh, Katelyn," Rosa said in a soft voice as she pulled the woman to her once more. Katelyn leaned her head on Rosa's shoulders and sobbed, seeming to be exhausted and quite beside herself. "Come in, now. Where are your things?"

"I didn't really bring anything with me besides my reticule. None of my clothes really fit me, and I just purchased whatever I felt I needed on the way," Katelyn explained as Rosa led her into her bedroom and closed the door behind them. Then Rosa encouraged Katelyn to lie down on her bed so she could help her out of her traveling boots. As Rosa did so, she found that Katelyn's feet were very swollen and red.

"Oh, my dear. Your feet look to be in pain," Rosa said as she placed a quilt over them and carefully tucked it in.

"I'm certain I will be fine once I rest for a bit. As you know, the train is awfully uncomfortable," Katelyn said as she began to close her eyes. Rosa could see that she was completely exhausted. Her mind was spinning when there was another knock on the door. With a sigh, Rosa got up from the side of the bed and opened the door to reveal Jacob.

"Thank goodness you are here," Rosa said as she grabbed Jacob's arm and pulled him into the room, making sure to leave the door completely open. "This is my good friend, Katelyn Trevino."

Jacob looked between the two women, trying to remember if Rosa had mentioned that her former charge was coming for their wedding. But when he saw that Katelyn was pregnant, he started to assume why Katelyn had come all this way.

"It's a pleasure to meet you, Miss Trevino. I'm Jacob Benning, Sheriff of Bear Creek, and Rosa's fiancé," Jacob said by way of introductions.

Katelyn smiled at him as she said, "I'm so glad that Rosa found someone to love after all." Her kind words made Rosa smile as she looked at Jacob. She was truly happy to be marrying him soon.

"I had just finished writing you a letter describing it all," Rosa said. "But what are you planning to do now that you're in Bear Creek?"

"All I want is to have this baby and raise it somewhere safe. The child and I would have been ruined in Boston. Perhaps here we could stand a chance at having a decent life," Katelyn explained. Rosa's heart hurt for her friend. She knew how Katelyn had been devastated when Fredrick had been promised in marriage to marry another. Now she understood just how deep that devastation ran.

"I promise you, Katelyn, that I'll take care of you. I won't let anyone ever treat you differently just because you had a baby out of wedlock," Rosa declared. She knew that even in Bear Creek there were many people who were prejudiced. But if she had any say in the matter, she would make sure Katelyn had a good chance at living a happy life with her child. She'd have to teach Katelyn a great deal about taking care of herself in this environment, but she knew that Katelyn was able to do anything once she put her mind to it.

"Why don't you get some rest," Jacob suggested. "You'll feel better after a proper nap." Katelyn simply nodded before she rolled onto her side and became as comfortable as she could. Rosa had never seen Katelyn in anything else but the most fashionable of gowns in expensive fabrics. Now it was strange to see her in a cotton traveling gown that looked too big for her.

Rosa followed Jacob out into the hallway and shut the door behind her. She sighed deeply, wondering what she was going to do about Katelyn.

"Well, it seems you'll have your best friend at our wedding," Jacob said with a small smile. Rosa loved how Jacob always looked on the bright side of things.

"That is true. But what could Katelyn possibly be thinking? I know her mother was quite overbearing, but Mr. Trevino has always been a very reasonable man. It makes me wonder if he even knows about Katelyn's condition," Rosa said.

"What do you want to do?" Jacob asked as he placed his good hand on Rosa's shoulder.

"Since you're a sheriff, could you send a telegram to Mr. Trevino in Boston? Just let him know that Katelyn has shown up in Bear Creek and that she's alright. She can stay with me till we get things figured out," Rosa suggested.

"I'm sure he'll appreciate knowing his daughter is safe," Jacob agreed. "I came to visit with you for a little bit. I know how busy you get in the evenings." Rosa smiled up at Jacob before she wrapped her arms around him, enjoying the feel of his body close to hers.

"Thank you," she said simply.

"You're welcome," Jacob said softly as he rested his head on top of hers, enjoying the sweet embrace. "I'll go send that telegram and then start thinking of a decent plan for Katelyn." Rosa let go of Jacob then and created a bit of space between them before they were spotted by Mr. Tibet. He was a very traditional man and probably wouldn't be too keen on seeing them hugging in the hallway alone.

"I truly appreciate it," Rosa said. "Are the Jenkins still coming for dinner tonight?"

"They sure are. Margret confirmed with me today when she came in to help Mrs. Fry with your wedding dress. I tried to sneak a peek while they were working and the women didn't appreciate that one bit," Jacob said with a chuckle. Rosa mock slapped Jacob on the left shoulder, making sure to avoid his bad one. Rosa knew that Dr. Harvey hadn't agreed to take the plaster off his arm just yet and that had made Jacob frustrated because he was determined not to get married with his arm in a sling.

"Well, I will see you back here for dinner. I can't wait to meet your friends," Rosa said as she rose onto her tiptoes and placed a quick kiss to Jacob's cheek before heading down the hallway to the kitchen. She needed to let Mrs. and Mr. Tibet know that they would be having an extra guest for some time.

CHAPTER 17

The weeks that went by after Katelyn had arrived in Bear Creek seemed to fly by as the wedding day approached. Rosa was thrilled to finally make Mathew and Jenny's acquaintance since they lived outside of town and had a small baby to tend to. But she could see why Mathew was Jacob's best friend by the way they teased one another. Katelyn had particularly taken a liking to Jenny since she was curious about what it was like to be a mother.

Now, the day had finally arrived. Rosa was in her bedroom at the inn as she began to get dressed in her wedding gown. Katelyn was with her as the two women had been sharing the bedroom. Rosa didn't mind since she knew that after the wedding she'd be moving into the Sheriff's apartment with Jacob. But it had been nice to have the company at night. Rosa could even imagine that she was sharing the room with her sister since she and Katelyn had spent so much time together growing up.

Katelyn helped Rosa into her wedding gown, and Rosa mused over the irony of it since it had been Rosa helping Katelyn dress since she was ten-years-old. Rosa saw herself in the looking glass once the gown was on and she could hardly believe how beautiful it was or how well it suited her. She then began working on her hair as she teased her golden curls into a stylish arrangement on the top of her head that left several tendrils hanging round her face to soften the effect. Then Katelyn helped her put on her veil.

"You look lovely," Katelyn said as she stepped back and studied Rosa. The last few weeks had been rough as Katelyn had to learn all manner of things that she wasn't used to doing for herself. In addition to the pregnancy, Katelyn was learning to cook and clean, as well as figuring out the best way to dress herself as her stomach continued to grow.

"It's so hard to think that this day has finally arrived. Weren't we just discussing me becoming a mail-order-bride the other day?" Rosa asked. The girls giggled and were then interrupted by a knock on the door. Katelyn went and opened it a peek. When she gasped, Rosa quickly turned to see what the matter was. Katelyn opened the door fully to reveal Mr. Trevino standing there.

"Father!" Katelyn exclaimed. "What are you doing here?"

"Once the Sheriff told me where you were, I came to see you immediately to make sure you were alright," Mr. Trevino said with tears in his eyes and looking very relieved. He stepped forward and wrapped his arms around his daughter. "Your mother had said you went to stay with a cousin. But when I got the Sheriff's telegram, I got the truth from her. Oh, Katelyn. I'm so sorry this happened to you." Father and daughter wept together as Rosa watched with a smile on her lips. She knew that Mr. Trevino would never abandon his daughter, and now she felt reassured over her decision to ask Jacob to send that telegram.

"It seems like important things are happening today," Mr. Trevino said as he cleared his throat and stepped back from Katelyn, his hand still on her shoulder and saw Rosa in all her glory.

"Rosa is getting married today," Katelyn explained with a bright smile. "Doesn't she look lovely?"

"She sure does," Mr. Trevino said with a nod. "I know it's unexpected, but I'd love to attend the wedding."

"Of course," Rosa said with a wide smile.

Once everyone's nerves were calmed down, Katelyn led Rosa from the bedroom and met Mr. and Mrs. Tibet in the foyer. Katelyn introduced them to her father and the older couple seemed delighted to know that he had come all the way from Boston to Bear Creek to be with his daughter. Together, the group made their way over to the town hall for the wedding ceremony. There Mr. Tibet was all prepared to lead Rosa down the aisle.

Jacob stood at the front of the town hall where Dan Mavis conducted his school lessons and Pastor Munster said his sermons once a month. They had arranged for the wedding to take place on one of the occasions that the Pastor was in town. Now, the guests were all seated and ready for the service. Mr. Tibet placed Rosa's hand on his arm and gently guided her up the aisle. As Jacob, standing in front of the preacher, looked at her approaching him in her beautiful wedding gown, his breath was taken away. He felt his heart pounding in his chest, full of love, as Rosa was brought to him. The ceremony itself seemed to go by in a blur as he looked down at the woman he loved and vowed to be her dutiful husband for the rest of their lives.

Rosa couldn't help but smile as Jacob kissed her soundly once they were pronounced man and wife. With that kiss, Rosa felt every unspoken promise that Jacob wanted her to know pass through in his public display of love. This was the start of her days with Jacob. Now they could begin a family of their own.

EPILOGUE

$\mathcal{D}$ear Rosa,

Things in Boston seem to have returned to normal. Little Rosa is toddling around the house now, getting into more things. She really keeps her nanny on her toes, but it's such a delight to see her growing. She babbles away and it won't be long before she'll actually be speaking proper words. I can't wait to hear what she says first..

How are you and Jacob doing? Any buns in the oven for you yet? Believe it or not, Mr. Kent Daniels has extended to me an offer of marriage. Seems the man has taken pity on me and wants Rosa to be raised with a proper mother and father. I figure that any man who can care for both me and my daughter is a keeper. That and he's also very wealthy and good looking to boot. We shall be married before the year is over.

Please write soon and tell me all about Bear Creek. My time there was short, but it will always hold a special place in my heart.

Yours truly,
Katelyn

. . .

ROSA SAT on the front porch of the Sheriff's Office in the rocker that Jacob had commissioned for her. Indeed, Rosa was starting to show that she was expecting and couldn't wait to write Katelyn and tell her all about it. After only four months of marriage Rosa was certain that she and Jacob would one day soon have a large family. If Dr. Harvey was correct, she'd be having twins at the beginning of spring.

Rosa was waiting up for Jacob after he rode up to visit with Brown Bear. The Indian Chief had wanted both Rosa and Jacob to attend so White Raven could give Rosa a blessing for her pregnancy. But since Rosa's feet had become very swollen, she hadn't spent much time traveling these days. As Jacob made his way across town, Rosa was able to spot him in the dim light of the lantern that she'd hung up. She waved at him as he came close, and he came and knelt beside her and wrapped both arms around her.

Just last week Dr. Harvey had finally taken the plaster off his arm. It was just in time for the cooler months of the year when he'd need a jacket or coat to keep him warm. It also felt good to hold his wife with both arms even though his right arm would still take time to gain back any muscle strength. But after having the plaster taken off, Jacob was confident that he'd regain his ability to shoot a gun.

"How are you doing?" Jacob asked as he leaned back.

"The same as when you left me. How is Brown Bear?" Rosa replied.

"He's good. He sends his congratulations on the pregnancy and wanted me to give you these," Jacob said. He withdrew a pair of moccasins from the small satchel that White Raven had sent him home with. Inside was also another small container that included more oil to help build strength in his arm. He helped Rosa out of her house slippers and put on the moccasins.

"They feel lovely," Rosa said as she wiggled her toes.

"Brown Bear explained that you'd be able to wear them everywhere, that they'll still protect your feet but give them room to grow," Jacob explained.

"Well, that was very kind of him." Jacob then helped Rosa to her feet and led her inside. He never grew tired of returning home to

Rosa. Though she still continued to help Mrs. Tibet at the inn with all the meals, every night was left to just them. He looked forward to every day together with Rosa and what the future would hold for them then.

The End

AMELIA'S OTHER BOOKS

Montana Westward Brides

CAST OF CHARACTERS

- **Jacob Benning**, Sheriff
- **Rosa Casey**
- Katelyn Trevino
- Tanner Williams, deputy
- Mathew & Jenny Jenkins, children: Michael (Mikey)
- Margret Phillips, Jenny's mother
- Mr. & Mrs. Fry, dry goods owner, seamstress
- Pastor Barthelme Munster, traveling pastor
- Mr. & Mrs. Tibet, inn owners and local restaurant/café
- Mr. Demetri Franklin, mayor of Bear Creek
- Louis Fritz, bank owner
- Curtis Denver, butcher
- Brown Bear, leader of the Sioux Indian camp
- Dan Mavis, schoolteacher and tutor
- Mitchel Franks, barber
- Dr. Harvey, local doctor
- Various ranchers, miners, homesteaders, and the local Sioux Indians

CONNECT WITH AMELIA

Visit my website at **www.ameliarose.info** to view my other books and to sign up to my mailing list so that you are notified about my new releases and special offers.

ABOUT AMELIA ROSE

Amelia is a shameless romance addict with no intentions of ever kicking the habit. Growing up she dreamed of entertaining people and taking them on fantastical journeys with her acting abilities, until she came to the realization as a college sophomore that she had none to speak of. Another ten years would pass before she discovered a different means to accomplishing the same dream: writing stories of love and passion for addicts just like herself. Amelia has always loved romance stories and she tries to tie all the elements she likes about them into her writing.

Made in the USA
Monee, IL
02 December 2020

50601309R00121